**GRAV**‗

MW01125531

Book 1

# THE DARK MAN

by
Desmond Doane

Publisher's Note: This is a work of fiction. Names, characters, places, and incidents are a product of the author's imagination. Locales and public names are sometimes used for atmospheric purposes. Any resemblance to actual people, living or dead, or to businesses, companies, events, institutions, or locales is completely coincidental.

ISBN-13: 978-1514677049
ISBN-10: 1514677040

The Dark Man / Desmond Doane. -- 1st ed.

*For those who bravely go into the night.*

# CHAPTER 1

A damp breeze pushes the rotting, translucent curtains to the side. A hundred years ago, they might have had some color. Someone's great-great-grandmother had undoubtedly hand-sewn them with pride and a song on her lips, humming as she swayed gently back and forth in her rocking chair.

Now, however, the curtains are just as faded and gray as everything else in this decrepit, abandoned farmhouse. Out here on the open land, miles away from the lights and sounds of Portland, Oregon, where it's buried under an overcast sky and the threat of rain, the night is as black as the bottom of a well.

It's hard to describe, but I feel as if my skin is starting to vibrate. That's a good sign. It means there's energy here. A presence. With the coming storm—lightning flashes in the distance, the rarest of occasions here—it'll help that much more. Those without a corporeal representation feed off nature's power; they gain strength from it, energy to communicate, and we may actually get some legitimate clues this evening. I felt that I was close the last time I was here, but it didn't happen. I went home with nothing but hours of blank tape and empty photographs, which was strange, since I was specifically asked to come here—you know, by a dead guy.

I have a new partner with me tonight. His name is Ulysses, officially, but I've decided on Ulie for short. He doesn't care what I call him. To Ulie, I'm the one and only Foodbringer. I'm the Light of His Life. I'm the One with the Stick. I am the Thrower of All Things.

I am Pillow. I am Chew Toy. I am He Who Takes Me for a Run Sometimes.

We've been together for a month, but this is the first time he's been on an investigation with me. Animals are sensitive to other realms, and I'm sure he'll be an excellent addition to my one-man team now that we've had an opportunity to connect on the appropriate levels. I went to the pound looking for company. I walked out of there with a friend.

My nose picks up on the fat scent of distant rain when another breeze rushes through the open window. Ulie lifts his head and sniffs the wind, too. Where I only smell impending precipitation, Ulie takes in the full breadth of life outside these walls. He cocks his head to the side, and I wonder what's pinging on his canine radar.

Ulie decides it's not worth more than a second of consideration. He looks up at me with an excited doggie grin, tongue wagging, almost like he's asking, "What's next, Ford? You brought me out here. Now what?"

I tell him, "Okay, Ulie, you're probably wondering why I brought you here, right?"

He closes his mouth. His ears perk up. He listens. He's probably waiting for a command, which will result in treats, but I like to pretend he's hanging on every word.

"Since it's your first day on the job, let me give you the quick and dirty. You know who sees things that other people don't? *Ghosts*."

We're standing in the second-floor hallway of this 150-year-old farmhouse, and at the mention of the word "ghosts," Ulie flicks his attention away from me, down to the distant end where the master bedroom sits empty and, I'll admit, menacing.

Could be nothing. Could be a mouse.

I don't spook easily. You can't in this line of work. And yet, there's something about this place—something about the energy I feel—that sets me on edge more than the other times I've been here. Perhaps I should say that it doesn't feel friendly.

It never has been, honestly. Tonight, though, it feels like this could be big.

My fingers go up to the crucifix necklace I wear on nights like this. I touch it, just to make sure it's there. I'm not religiously religious, but I'm happy to call Jesus my copilot when it feels necessary.

I say to Ulie, "We're not actually on a case tonight, my friend. This is different, okay? We're looking for . . . well, we're looking for our own answers. If this works out, maybe you can start coming along with me on jobs, yeah? Local ones, at least."

Ulie grumble-whines and shakes his head, paws at his snout.

"That's easy," I say, answering an unasked question. "If you want to solve a mystery with no *living* witnesses, my dear flop-eared pal, then you have to talk to the *dead* ones."

When he turns his quizzical gaze up to me, he mutters something in dog-speak and prances in place as if he's anxious. His eyes go from me to the master bedroom and back again.

"You want to go take a peek?" I ask.

He snorts his approval and takes three tentative steps in that direction, looks back and waits, tail wagging hesitantly.

I start to say something to him, then chuckle to myself, realizing that my life has become the plot of a Carter Kane novel. It's not a bad thing by any means—Kane is a master of paranormal suspense and part of the reason I'm so fascinated with what's *out there*. He shaped my early years after many, many long, sleepless nights reading his work. And here I am, investigating the mystical with a highly intelligent mutt, having what appears to be a reciprocal conversation.

Kane would be proud.

Ulie takes another faltering step down the hallway. He barks once. It's not much, nothing more than a warning shot across the bow. I've heard him attempt to be more vicious with a butterfly that spooked him, but still, his caution lifts the hair on my arms.

"You think he's in there, boy?" I ask, kneeling beside the brave pup.

The *he* in question—I've spoken to him before. Carefully. I was warned before I came here. I've handled worse; you gotta be careful, though, no matter what.

My equipment case sits on the floor at my feet. It's about the size of a vintage suitcase from the 1970s, could probably double as a life raft built for two, and inside, it's packed with hard but forgiving foam where carved slots hold the items I need to conduct a proper paranormal investigation.

For a brief moment, I lament the fact that I'm down to this. One single case with five to ten devices, depending on the location and what options seem to work best after an initial analysis.

I miss my team. I miss the cameras and the cameramen. I miss investigating a single place for a week to create an hour-long slot. I even miss my producer, Carla Hancock, who was ultimately responsible for the show's demise.

"Miss" is a strong word for Carla. Perhaps it's better to say I have faint memories of the good times.

I'll never be able to explain why I let her talk me into using a five-year-old girl as a trigger object, which is something those of us in the paranormal world employ to entice spirits into communication.

Maybe it was greed. Maybe it was the thrill of the hunt. Maybe it was the potential for massive exposure. *"Tonight on this very special, live-on-Halloween episode of* Graveyard: Classified, *be prepared to witness history."*

You know how they say there's no such thing as bad press?

Apparently there are exceptions to every rule.

*Graveyard: Classified* was the number-one show on cable during the coveted eight-to-nine slot on Thursday nights. We outranked every major network three-to-one. We even had more viewers than that super popular sitcom with the snippy part-time waitress who couldn't possibly afford that gorgeous loft apartment in New York City.

Top o' the world, we were.

And then, little Chelsea Hopper crawled into an attic and fell out with three massive claw marks along her cheek, neck, and collarbone. The entire crew, and millions of viewers at home and online, all heard the demonic growl during the live broadcast.

I checked. The attic was empty of anything living.

Chelsea's claw marks were real. She still bears the scars.

*Graveyard: Classified* wasn't picked up for its eleventh season after that, and it drifted off into the land of late-night reruns—the spirits of once-popular shows.

For the record, I questioned Carla, and myself, over that decision every step of the way, right up until the director turned the cameras on. I knew better, and I still regret it. I send care packages to the address where Chelsea lives, but I have no way of knowing if she ever gets them. Her parents did sign a contract, after all, and were awarded an incredible amount once the glory-seeking lawyers were able to find loopholes in it—yet, understandably, the Hoppers haven't chosen to forgive those who put their daughter in danger, including themselves, I bet.

A long, deep breath pushes those memories away. I choose an electromagnetic field detector—EMF for short—and a digital voice recorder, two of the simplest tools in my arsenal and often some of the best ways to detect an otherworldly presence. You almost always want to take a baseline reading with an EMF detector to make sure that there's nothing to contaminate your investigation like faulty wiring and things like that, but I figure out here, in this old farmhouse that used to be lit by candles and lanterns, there's no need.

Ulie prances some more, waiting patiently while I turn on both devices and perform one last equipment check.

The EMF detector reads "0.0" on the digital display. If it spikes while it measures the area within range, it'll give me an idea that there's something in the room making use of the available energy—energy from me, energy from the batteries in my equipment, energy from the lightning that's crawling closer.

The digital voice recorder detects what we call EVPs. Electronic Voice Phenomena, which are sounds—and voices—that aren't detectable by the human ear. Back in the olden days, and I'm talking, like, six months ago and earlier, we would run the digital recorders for hours, and then have to spend an equal amount of time reviewing the files on the back end of an investigation.

Now, however, with the BR-4000 I'm currently holding, you can do a live-stream listen. If I ask a question and something responds, I'll immediately hear it through my earbuds, rather than having to sit in my office, listening to hours of my heavy breathing, footsteps, and repetitive questions. It's a necessary evil if I'm investigating a larger place, like a hospital or warehouse, and have to run multiple DVRs at once. It can be dull, yeah, but that potential for an amazing discovery is always right around the corner.

Okay, so, with my EMF detector on and reading baseline zeroes, and the BR-4000 earbuds in and registering the ambient noise, which now includes Ulie's claws clicking on the hardwood floor, we march forward with tentative footsteps, one shoe and paw in front of the other.

Honestly, I haven't been this nervous in a while. I've been here twice. The first time, I caught two Class-A EVPs—the top of the quality charts—that spooked me to the core: "*I know what you want*," and "*Chelsea . . .Hopper.*" Both came from a deep, guttural male voice, angry and malevolent, within five minutes of each other, and I captured them in the master bedroom. After another half hour of fruitless questioning, I'd said, "If you'd like me to leave, give me a sign."

I asked for it, and I got it. I watched as a rotting two-by-four rose straight up off the floor and stood there, like a soldier at attention, for a full five seconds before it launched itself across the bedroom and missed my head by less than a foot.

The second time I was here, nothing happened. Not a damn thing. I sat and walked and perched and squatted and napped in this godforsaken place all night, alone, waiting on something to come back and challenge me again. Nothing but dead, boring silence.

Tonight, though . . . yeah, it feels different. He's here, and I plan to get some answers out of him.

These days, it's rare that I'm able to get out and investigate for fun. Now that *Graveyard: Classified* has basically gone the way of its own name, I have plenty of money that accompanies a guilty conscience; the latter keeps me from disappearing to a beach hut in the South Pacific. I can't just walk away from this life. There are promises to keep and wrongs to avenge.

What I do is, I work freelance, trying my best to assist police departments in investigations, both fresh and cold cases, in turn helping families find answers that were buried with their kin. When it comes to family matters like what a loved one intended in a will, or when it comes to proof in an ongoing investigation, paranormal evidence hasn't been officially or legally cleared for use. However, it often gives those involved enough clues or hints to proceed appropriately.

I do that kind of work to cherish the relief that I see in a stumped detective or a worried family member's eyes, and I haven't decided if I'm selfishly or selflessly building up karma.

This kind of investigation, what I'm doing here tonight, has nothing to do with an ongoing case.

It has everything to do with little Chelsea Hopper.

A ghostly messenger residing here requested me by name, and I think some of my answers may be on the other side of that bedroom door.

# CHAPTER 2

I had to hop on a flight early the next morning, and a day later, after some much-needed rest, I'm sitting here in a stuffy office that could double as a gym sauna.

The detective's suit doesn't fit him well. One of these days, I may introduce him to Melanie, who used to be the head of wardrobe before *Graveyard: Classified* was cancelled. She'd know exactly how to dress him properly, maybe give the poor guy an upright, professional appearance, rather than this slump-shouldered, slept-in-his-suit look he's rolling with now. Realistically, he's probably in his late forties, though the impression he gives off is, "I'm missing Bingo night and *Matlock* reruns, you whippersnapper."

He says to me, "This stuff is legit, right? What you do?"

I get this question often enough that it doesn't bother me anymore.

Maybe a little bit.

I tell him, "I've seen crap you wouldn't believe, Detective Thomas. I've watched chairs slide across rooms by themselves. I've seen an indentation form in a couch cushion, just like somebody sat down beside me to watch the big game. I've had my hair pulled, scratches and burns all over my body, cabinets flung open, knives flying at my head . . ."

"I remember, definitely. I was a big fan of *Graveyard*, back when it was still on. I just thought, you know . . ."

"That we made it all up?"

"Hate to say it, but yeah. Special effects are so good these days. I don't mean to accuse you or anything, but some of those shenanigans . . . a bit hard to swallow."

"Come with me one night. I'll show you firsthand. You guys do ride-alongs, right? Same thing."

He holds up a palm and gives me a fake frown. "Thanks, I'm good. Better for me that it stays on the other side of the TV screen. I've seen enough on *this* side of the grave to keep me awake at night."

I'm here in Virginia Beach, Virginia, this week. The VBPD called me in to see if I could do anything about this cold-case murder that recently popped back up in the national spotlight when an explicit diary was uncovered.

Apparently, the former mayor had been having an affair with his secretary—go figure—and after she floated to the surface at the mouth of the Chesapeake Bay ten years ago, nobody considered him a suspect. Mayor Gardner passed away back in 2012, according to Detective Thomas, and without any further leads, the diary was pretty much useless. There was proof of an affair in pasty, white, fleshy, gray-haired detail, but *not* proof that he murdered her, or hired someone to do it, after Louisa Craghorn threatened blackmail, the details of which she described in the final entry.

Before she was murdered, Louisa was young—thirty-two at the time—Filipina, and loved her Pomeranian. She liked taking a pottery class on Thursday nights and ran six miles four days a week. She had been married to her husband, Dave Craghorn, for just under two years when Mayor Gardner approached her about a promotion.

And, evidently, the stipulations included an inappropriate relationship, considering he had been married to the same woman for forty-nine years. She's alive and well, and also happens to be quite the public socialite around the Hampton Roads area. Ellen Gardner is still sparkling in her early seventies and loves to entertain guests, and from what Detective Thomas says, the diary revelation hasn't slowed her down in the slightest.

Detective Thomas clears his throat and takes a sip of steaming coffee. "You want some?" He holds the mug higher and tells me, "Should warn you, folks around here make it strong enough for a spoon to stand upright."

"As delicious as that sounds, I'm good. Had my fair share already." I lean back in the uncomfortable chair across from him and cross my legs. "So you explained some of the history on the phone, Detective. What're we looking at here and how do you think I can help?"

"Straight down to business. My kinda guy." He picks up a file box that's stuffed to the rim with folders and clasp envelopes. "This is the Craghorn case history. Or, well, I should say that it's the start of it. There are four more in our file room downstairs. And . . . now it might be more appropriate to call it the Craghorn-Gardner case."

My eyebrows arch at the sheer amount of it all, and my head ricochets backward like I just bumped it on a low doorway. "That much, huh?"

"Tell me about it."

"You had *that much* evidence, and the case still went cold?"

He pulls a shoulder up along with the corner of his mouth. "It happens. Sometimes you just . . . sometimes the bloodhound loses the trail."

I nod and clasp my fingers, then lean in on my elbows. Once in a while, I have to play the role of *human* investigator to get at the root of what someone is really looking for. It helps when I switch to my normal role of paranormal investigator.

I ask the detective, "What were you going to say there, just now? You stopped yourself."

The telephone on his desk rings loudly. He ignores it in favor of staring at me, waiting as if he's trying to decide how to answer.

That is, how to answer *me*, not the phone.

Five rings pass before he picks up the receiver and immediately slams it back down, hanging up on his clueless caller. "Sometimes," he says, "you just give up. I hate to admit it, but after you've exhausted every possible option, after you've got a few more gray hairs and the bags under your eyes look like they're carrying bowling balls, you have to admit defeat. Sometimes, the bad guys get away with it, Mr. Ford."

"Understandable. Who was the lead on the case back in '04? Is that detective still around?"

Detective Thomas raises his hand, almost sheepishly, without saying a word.

"You? I didn't think active homicide detectives tackled cold-case investigations. Or is that just an assumption I made up?"

"Once Elaine Lowe—that's the surviving husband's housekeeper—once she came forward with the diary she found, I requested this assignment. Immediately dropped everything I was working on because I wanted another shot, and here I am, six months later, no closer than I was back in 2004. New evidence, a new list of suspects who were cleared, and a whole lot uglier." He sighs as he flips a folder closed and drops it on his desk.

"And murder was your original conclusion way back when?"

He nods, grimaces when he sips his steaming hot coffee.

"I read the content you sent me, Detective, but from what I gathered, the body had, uh, it had decayed so much that you weren't quite sure."

He grins at me. "Then you didn't read all of it."

He's got me there. I didn't, because when he called and asked me to hop on the next flight to Norfolk International, I was bone weary after the third farmhouse investigation. The events of two nights ago had prevented sleep from coming easily, and I'm dying to get back there to follow up, but the karma ain't going to refill itself.

Part of the idea is, I feel like if I do enough of these investigations, I could look at pitching a new show idea to some producers who may be willing to overlook the fallout from the demise of *Graveyard: Classified*, but until I'm ready for that day, I'm not about to step back into prime time until I can find some peace for Chelsea Hopper, and in turn, myself. What I caught the other night could lead to a breakthrough even though I haven't had time to fully analyze its meaning.

Ulie hasn't been the same, either. The only thing I can do from here, three thousand miles away, is hope that my ex-wife, the aforementioned Melanie from wardrobe, is taking good care of him. She reports a tucked tail and whimpering, but he's finally eating again.

I say to Detective Thomas, "Guilty as charged. Although that's probably not the best thing to say to a cop, huh?"

Thankfully, he snickers. If I can get away with bad jokes, we might have a decent working relationship. Given what I do, it helps if my clients are easygoing and have an open mind. Judging by the fact that I'm here already, he's either willing to try or has crossed the DMZ into desperation.

"You're off the hook, Mr. Ford. I sent a lot, I know. Anyway, so, whenever a *naked* body pops up in the water, you suspect what?"

"Homicide. But if she was clothed, then my first thought would be an accident or suicide."

"Exactly. Could be the natural wear of the currents pulling her clothes off, but more than likely, she comes out like that, she went in like that. When her husband had reported her missing, the guys looked for her and came up with nothing. Missing Persons monitored her credit cards and bank accounts because sometimes these women—or men—they get into drugs, or they just want to be gone.

Maybe they finally leave an abusive relationship behind, or they ran off with the gardener—or in this case, the Gardner. Pardon the pun."

His ambivalence doesn't sit well in my gut, but I suppose after all he's seen, it's just another day on the assembly line.

"And you found something that told you otherwise?" I ask.

"Upon deeper inspection, once the ME got past all the—you know what? I'm going to spare you the wet details. The contusions around her neck showed signs of strangulation. At first glance, you might have suspected it could have been something underwater. Seaweed. Stray rope from an anchor. Maybe she's out skinny-dipping, knocks her head against a rock, she sinks, the current drags her into something, and that's all she wrote."

"I'm guessing that wasn't the case."

"You'd be guessing correctly. The bruises revealed what we consistently see in these types of murders, and that's a really strong grip." Detective Thomas cups his hands around an invisible neck, and I have to say, it freaks me out when he grinds his teeth as if he's actually performing the act itself. I've battled demons with a crucifix, side by side with terrified clergymen, but this gives me serious goosebumps. It's almost like he's—never mind. I'm on edge after the other night. It's nothing.

"Were you able to tell, say, the size of the hands, or maybe the strength of the squeeze? Meaning, like, male or female?"

"Trust me, Mr. Ford, we went over all that during the preliminary investigations. That's the simple stuff. If you catch the deceased at the proper time, you might have a better chance of determining something like that on a good day while pulling a few miracle cards, but not after a body has been in the bay for over a week. We were lucky the ME was able to come up with what he did."

I sit back in my chair and put my finger to my lips, thinking. I'm not necessarily or inherently built with the deductive reasoning skills of a seasoned detective, but more than once, I've come up with an angle that helped spark their creative thought processes before I ever set foot in an investigation site. Beginner's luck, I guess. Often a baffled, desperate police department has begrudgingly brought me in at the request of someone at the station who was a fan of the show, and frequently, the spirits of "the deceased," as Detective Thomas refers to them, are uncooperative. I can't *make* them talk any more than I can make a proper omelet on a regular basis. If it ain't in the cards, it ain't happening that day.

I still charge them for my time. The way I see it, detectives go to work every day and don't solve cases, yet they still get paid. I could easily do this work pro bono, no problem, but I've found that if someone is paying me, they're far more likely to be reasonable and accommodating.

I stop and start a few sentences. I come up with nothing, not a single approach that I think Detective Thomas can check out. He tried it all. He's been trying again for the last six months, which means we're down to my last line of questioning for him.

"Then that leaves us here," I say, sitting up straighter. "A lot of times PDs will call me in for the novelty of it. They're out of options, and they think, 'Oh, what the hell, this guy works for peanuts. Why don't we give him a try?' I don't like those. I'm not saying you *are* one of those, I'm just saying it's hard walking onstage where the crowd hasn't been warmed up first. See what I'm saying?"

He taps a pencil against his cheek and acknowledges me by dipping his chin.

"Then, other times, some detective has seen something he can't explain and wants a second opinion, which I'm happy to help with. Those are great. It means there might be something there, and we might already have a solution to work toward. Even rarer still are guys like you, the ones who call with a little extra edge to their voices, the ones who are hesitant to say exactly *why* they're calling. Guys who are nothing but curious? They'll admit it right away. They'll say, 'This weird thing happened; we want you to come check it out.' But detectives like you, been at this twenty years or more, seen everything there is to see, all the evil in humanity . . . you don't need me. You got new evidence, fresh clues. You're not ready to throw in the towel after six months, Detective. I don't believe it when you say you're back to where you started. You called me here for a reason. Something spooked you. So let me ask you this: What was it? What did you see?"

"I'll never forget it," he answers with that somber tone I've come to recognize so well.

# CHAPTER 3

We're standing in front of the Craghorn residence. It's too damn hot in the Hampton Roads area this time of year, and I can feel the sweat beading up in places where I don't enjoy being swampy. It's part of the gig, though, and I agreed to let Detective Thomas explain himself here rather than back at the station. He said it would make more sense if Dave Craghorn, husband of the deceased, was there to back him up.

Detective Thomas tucks his hands into his pockets and looks up at the top floor of the three-story home. We're over in Portsmouth, a small city adjacent to Virginia Beach, where some of the residences are centuries old, built back when the masons didn't mind stacking stones thirty or forty feet in the air on all sides. These things were built to last.

The detective admires it, head tilted, back angled as we look up toward the hand-carved molding along the eaves. He says, "Beautiful place, ain't it?"

I lie to him and say yeah, it's nice, while I try to see it through his eyes. I get what he's saying; the place has a strong presence. It's bulky and broad-shouldered, reminds me of a middle linebacker, but I don't really see the *beauty* in it, per se. To me, it's a giant collection of rocks and cement that's covered in moss with vines climbing up the sides. Maybe it's because, over the years, too many houses have become enemies to me, burdened with evil, demonic spirits that torture families and drive them from the place where they wanted to live out their dreams. Instead, they suffer through nightmares.

So, yeah. Houses? I don't really trust them, not until I've had a chance to get to know one. Mine back in Portland, high up on the hill overlooking the Willamette River, has had so many incantations, prayers, and positive vibes bestowed upon it that you might as well say it's guarded by a soothing, white light that envelops the whole thing. That's my sanctuary, the place where I retreat after I've battled with the darkness.

Not every house that's haunted is black on the inside, just like not every spirit is a demonic, evil entity. Sometimes it's somebody's sweet old grandma who never got a chance to say goodbye before she left this world, and once I help her with that, the fog lifts.

Point is, until I know what I'm dealing with, I approach each place—each home, each train station, each barn, whatever—with full shields, and every now and then, if I've come out unscathed, I'll take a moment to appreciate the architecture, but not until I know I'm going home without any unwanted guests tagging along.

The detective clears his throat, and I can hear a bit of emotion in there, like he's trying to cough it up and maybe swallow it, down where the rest of his feelings stay buried.

I ask, "You okay?"

"Yeah," he croaks, then looks past me down the sidewalk. "There's Craghorn. I won't go in there without him, and to be honest, I don't know how he lives here by himself."

Pardon the expression, but I'm *dying* to know what happened here. After all these years and literally a thousand investigations, I still don't feel like I've seen everything there is to see, at least when it comes to the paranormal world.

I still get confused, spooked, scared, excited, and thrilled when something—notice I said some*thing*—reaches out from the other side. You'd think I'd be desensitized by now, but the truth is, this shit will never get old for me.

There's the job, then there's the wonder.

Detective Thomas doesn't smile when he lifts a hand, waves to Dave Craghorn and says, "Good to see you again, Dave. Thanks for doing this."

Dave offers a morose smile as fake as the day is long, and we shake hands. He's somewhere in his mid-forties, a little older than me, with long salt-and-pepper hair and a matching goatee that extends down past his Adam's apple. His tan jacket hangs loosely on his shoulders, like it might have fit one day, but now it's nothing more than a piece of clothing draped over shoulders as thin as a wire hanger. Which, of course, adds another layer to his odd vibe. It's gotta be well over ninety degrees out here and 100 percent humidity. He has to be swimming in that thing.

He says, "Nice of you to come, Mr. Ford. Big fan of your old show." It's a flat, emotionless voice, no heft to it at all, like he's a prisoner who's afraid to speak up in front of his captors.

"Happy to help," I respond, studying him. Let me just say this: I take my B-list fame with a grain of salt. I've been to the big parties and hobnobbed with the elites of entertainment, but I've never been one to abuse the privileges of celebrity. I'm lucky and I know it. I don't throw my soup in waiters' faces, I don't whine and complain when I'm not given the best table, nor when I actually have to *wait* for a table just like everyone else. That said, I can always tell when someone has no idea who I am, or has never seen an episode of *Graveyard: Classified*, or more than likely, just doesn't give a shit. In fact, I think I appreciate the latter the most. It allows me to investigate a site on level grounds.

Dave lifts a shaking finger, pointing up the tall set of stairs as he mumbles, "It's, um, it's right up there."

"Here we go." Detective Thomas groans, pauses in midstep, and pushes bravely forth.

Not really, but I have to give the guy credit. Whatever happened in there spooked him all to hell, and he's going anyway. I follow him up, taking the steps in twos, with Dave Craghorn following us both. I glance over my shoulder and he's climbing the steps as if each foot is encased in cement—big, heavy blocks that he struggles with as he pushes himself onward, one after the other. I can almost hear the thick clunk with each step. He's dreading this just as much as Detective Thomas is, and I feel for him. Poor guy comes home to this every single day.

The front door is thick wood, painted a shade of cloudy gray that seems to fit perfectly with the gloom and doom motif of this place. Craghorn's key makes a deep, metallic thunk, reminding me of a jailer in an ancient castle dungeon, and I immediately feel the cold of the interior racing out as the door swings inward.

Detective Thomas shivers.

Now I know why Craghorn is wearing the jacket. He says, "It's always like this now. The cold never leaves my bones. It follows me."

I don't shiver from the temperature. I do it because of the defeat in his voice.

He adds, "Come on in. Might want to say a little prayer first, if you're the religious sort."

Out of habit, my fingers go up to the crucifix dangling at my chest. It feels warmer than usual against my skin. I'm not sure if that's a good sign.

Craghorn stares down the hallway, and Detective Thomas follows with a resigned grunt. "To serve and protect," he says.

As soon as I step across the threshold, I feel it. Not just the cold, but what's buried within it. Remorse. Loss. Regret.

And so much anger.

I pause because it's been a while since I've felt such a . . . *presence* right away. Not since the Alexander house six months ago, the one up in Lansing, Michigan, with the pissed-off spirit of an ex-con who was haunting a young single mother and her three children. She'd sent me a pleading e-mail, and once in a while, I'll take on a special case pro bono, because when it comes to kids, I simply can't let that go. It's why I'm still battling with what happened to Chelsea Hopper.

This, whatever it is, actually feels stronger than the ghost of Delmar Jackson, and that's saying a lot. It took me, three Catholic priests, and enough holy water to fill a bathtub to get him gone.

My goosebumps get goosebumps. No matter how many times I've done this, the chill of evil prickles my skin. It's not the fiery, burning, licking flames of hell like the Bible and your Sunday pastor would have you believe.

Evil is the darkness. It's the cold.

It's the absence of love and light.

"Ford," says Detective Thomas, leaning back into the hallway, "you coming?"

"Yeah, sorry. Just getting a feel for the house."

"And?"

"You were right. This place is *dark*."

***

Craghorn sits on a sofa that looks like it might have been purchased at a yard sale in 1973. In fact, I'm fairly certain that my parents had this exact same couch with the exact same pattern in our living room back when Nixon was in office. Instinctively, I look at the far left cushion to see if the hot chocolate stain is there. My sister, Amy, spooked me with a Halloween mask when I was nine. The contents of the steaming mug went all over me, her, and the couch, and left behind a brown memory that refused to go away no matter how much we scrubbed.

It's not there, by the way, but surveying the couch does give me a chance to check out Craghorn some more while we wait on Detective Thomas to emerge from the bathroom. I can't tell if Craghorn is a small man in general, or if he's *making* himself smaller, like he's trying to hide from something. Or it could be the fact that the springs and cushions are so worn out on his couch that the damn thing is trying to swallow him whole.

I decide on a combination of all three and lean in with my elbows on my knees, asking him, "Lots of nice things here. You decorate the place yourself?" It's such a pointless, baseline question that I'm not even sure why I asked it. I think maybe I'm simply trying to fill up the sucking void in here that's taking every ounce of energy out of this room. I hear the toilet flush down the hallway and say a silent thanks. As good as I can be with people at times—you have to be in this line of work—Craghorn seems more comfortable around Detective Thomas. He hasn't said a word since the detective excused himself.

Craghorn flits a hand around the room and blandly answers, "Most of it belonged to my wife. She won't let me get rid of anything."

Present tense. *Won't let me.* It's a clear hint regarding his feelings about the situation, though I can't yet tell if he's hanging on to the past or if he means her spirit is here and dictating what does and does not go out with the garbage.

He adds, "And, really, it's all part of the scenery now. I barely notice."

Detective Thomas walks back into the living room, giving one final swipe across his mouth. I'm sure I heard retching while he was in there, or what it sounds like when someone is holding it back. His skin has turned a pasty white, and there's no life in his eyes.

"What?" he snaps when he catches me looking at him.

"Nothing. You just . . . you look like you've seen a ghost." I fake a laugh. I can't tell you how many times I've tried that joke just to lighten the mood before an investigation. I can count on one hand how many times it's actually worked over the past decade, yet it doesn't stop me from trying.

Thankfully, Craghorn snickers, and now I can graduate to counting on two hands.

I continue, trying to sound upbeat between the fearful shaking of Detective Thomas and the morose gloom of Dave Craghorn. What they're projecting doubles the effect of the blackness billowing into this room. "Normally, this is the part where I'd start out with a line of questioning to sorta gather up the history about what's going on with your property. Everybody has a story, right? Even those who have moved on. But since you, Mr. Craghorn, didn't necessarily ask me for help, and since Detective Thomas did, I'm going to let him paint the picture, and we'll go from there, okay?"

Craghorn nods without making eye contact. He almost reminds me of a witness for the prosecution who is too afraid to say yes, too afraid to point out the bad man in the room. Instead, he's focused on his fingernails and what's underneath them, and makes no further attempt at communication. His shallow breathing and a knee that bounces like chattering teeth on a cold day are enough to reveal his anxiety.

Detective Thomas coughs into his fist and then cups his hands. He blows into them, trying to warm them up and then rubs his palms together. He huffs a fat breath of air, like he's expecting it to plume. It doesn't, and he almost seems perplexed.

Cold spots are another sign of a potential spiritual presence. Normally, it's nothing more than a chilly area in the center of a warm room, maybe five, ten, fifteen degrees cooler than the ambient temperature. It's where a spirit is absorbing energy, hoping to compile enough to communicate with the living.

Craghorn's entire house feels like a meat locker.

The detective's next words drop the temperature even further.

# CHAPTER 4

## CHELSEA HOPPER
### TWO YEARS AGO
### A Very Special Live Halloween Episode

"*Ford*," said Mike Long, my fellow lead investigator, "you absolutely can*not* use that little girl as a trigger object. How many times do I have to tell you? And fuck me, man, here we are! Again! It's too dangerous, like, off-the-charts dangerous. You and I both know how sensitive children are to these things. You *know* this. And at five years old? She's immaculate on the inside. There are no footprints in the mud of her mind." He said this last bit with force, tapping the side of his head as he accentuated each syllable.

Carla Hancock, my producer, put her hand on Mike's shoulder and nudged him back, just enough to distance him from the circle of trust that she was trying to establish. Carla, Don Killian, Gavin Probst, and Timothy Shearing, all of my producers and co-producers, the directors, the sound guys, the whole lot of them were crowded around me. *Graveyard: Classified* had about four minutes before the live-feed broadcast began for what promised to be the biggest, most-watched paranormal investigation ever.

Carla said, "I don't need to remind you that we're going live in forty-seven countries, do I? *Millions* of people are watching, Ford, and they want a show. They want the goddamn Super Bowl of paranormal investigations, and if you want to keep this freight train rolling, you'll send her in there."

I shook my head. I felt the regret and remorse encroaching on my gut. I felt like, if I did it, if I really bent to Carla's will and sent a five-year-old child into an attic, to face a demon, alone, then my soul would turn as black as the creature we were hunting.

But the ratings. My God, the ratings. Astronomical.

Rob and Leila Hopper stood off to the side, near the catering truck, giving Chelsea bites of ice cream and pieces of the peppermint candy that Mike always requested before every shoot. They'd agreed to this because . . . well, one, we were offering them more money for a single night in their house than Rob earned in a year as a customer support technician. They weren't filled with bloodlust or anything like that. They weren't demented, crazy freaks that got their jollies by torturing their daughter. They weren't pageant parents who subjected their child to psychological trauma before she could even spell it.

There was none of that. They were good people, and I knew that because I'd had extensive discussions with them. They just happened to live in the Most Haunted House in America for three terrifying years after Chelsea was born. Chelsea experienced more paranormal activity in those three years than I had my entire career.

So why were her parents sending her in there? Because Carla went behind my back and convinced them that having Chelsea confront the demon would be the best way to get rid of her traumatic memories once and for all. I nearly walked away when I found out. I should've, but I didn't.

I had contractual obligations and, admittedly, once I thought about it for a little while, Carla's arguments *almost* made sense.

We were minutes away from going live, knowing there would be millions of people around the world who would judge, hate, condemn, and trash the Hoppers all over social media. They'd label them horrible parents. They'd say there was no way in hell that any self-respecting person would ever do that to a child, especially their own offspring. They'd type in all caps at them for being idiots, and likely call social services in an attempt to have Chelsea taken away. They'd tell their friends that the Hoppers were horrible, detestable, greedy human beings who were only in it for the money.

The Hoppers had hundreds of reasons to change their minds, and every single one of them was the best one. We were offering them a ton of money, yeah, but there was more to it than that.

Agreeing to something so completely ridiculous sounds insane, right? True, but think about it from their perspective.

You try watching your daughter go through what Chelsea experienced for three years and what she suffered through every night in her dreams; you try saying no when someone approaches you with promises of redemption, vengeance, and relief. Imagine having a nasty, unbearable toothache every day of your life. You can't eat. You can't sleep. You can't take a nice, long drink of cool water without blinding pain screaming throughout your body. And then one day, a nice lady with an enchanting smile shows up at your front door and says, "I've got a magic pill that'll fix what ails you. All you have to do is swallow it, and your troubles will be over. It doesn't cost anything, and, as a matter of fact, we'll *pay you* to take it."

Would you do it? Would you take the pill?

As a parent, if it were your daughter who was in pain, would you take the chance?

I'd thought about this for weeks. Mike and I argued night after night leading up to the investigation, and he was still arguing with me mere minutes before we went on air. I'd met privately with the Hoppers and explained to them what we were going up against, and they knew, they understood. The worst part about it was, they said that they trusted me, that they knew I wouldn't let anything happen to their little girl. They knew Chelsea was the vanguard in a horrifying war, and that she would win because I'd be by her side. They believed that, and I didn't try to convince them otherwise.

Why not?

If . . . no, *when* she came out the victor, I originally believed that this single investigation would seal our place in paranormal history and in television ratings. Rich corporations would lock us into sponsorships and contracts lasting as long as we wanted them to.

Big Burger City. Tire Monster. Avocado Giant.

They were all standing by with ink pens and glimmers in their eyes.

Rob and Leila trusted me, but I had to wonder, did I trust myself to do the right thing? I don't know.

I had about a minute thirty to change my mind, which was insane, because it was right before we investigated the Most Haunted House in America on a Very Special Live Halloween Episode. I still had a chance to back out.

Decisions, decisions. Devil. Angel.

Nobody but the crew and the Hoppers knew what the surprise was for the viewing audience. I had it all figured out. If I changed my mind, I would just switch up the intro and catch *everyone* off guard, including the producers and directors. The unassuming house in that quaint little neighborhood on the eastern side of Cleveland, Ohio, could be the surprise all by itself, with no need to include an innocent child.

*You'd never guess it, America, but this beautiful bungalow, on this quiet street where children play and puppies dance, is a place of such unimaginable horror, that I—me—Ford Atticus Ford, am terrified to go inside.*

I didn't have to mention the Hoppers at all, and they understood that this was a possibility. I'd promised to cut them a check from my own bank account if I ripped up their contract in the final seconds. I couldn't leave them hanging once I learned that they planned to set up a college fund for Chelsea with the money they earned from the show.

An intern with a clipboard, an earpiece, and a puffy mic curled around in front of her lips darted over to us and tapped Carla on the shoulder. "One minute, twenty seconds, Miss Hancock."

"Thanks, Ambrosia."

Mike threw his hands in the air and backed away, shaking his head. "I can't do it, Ford. I can't. *We* can't. We're going to burn for this." He stopped his retreat and locked his fingers at the base of his skull. "Actually, you know what? *You're* going to burn for this. I'm done." He said this with all the conviction he could muster, but he didn't go anywhere. He knew that Carla Hancock had the power to ruin his career. Despite his reservations about the investigation, he loved what he did, and to have that and the money taken away . . .

Carla said to me, "Don't listen to him. You're a professional. You're a *warrior*, and we're going to make cable television *history*. You, Ford, *you* will be Monday morning's water-cooler discussion for a long, *long* time."

"Carla, I—"

"Do it for *her*," Carla said, pointing at the bouncy, happy, ponytailed child who barely had any idea what was coming next. All Chelsea knew was that her parents had brought her back to where she used to live and they wanted her to go with Mr. Ford to talk to the dark man. Aside from that, it was fun seeing all these people around. To her, it was a party.

Chelsea slurped the chocolate ice cream off her cone and giggled when Rob tried to sneak a bite. Carla pointed, adding, "Give that little girl some peace. Get her life back."

"She looks fine to me," I replied, but it was only because she had candy, ice cream, and a horde of people paying attention to her. It was a weak defense. I knew that

Chelsea had been plagued by terrifying dreams, constantly waking up, screaming and crying.

Ambrosia, the intern, nudged Carla with a little extra insistence and said, "Twenty seconds, Miss Hancock."

"Ford?"

"What?"

"You heard her. What's it going to be?"

"I—"

"*Beat* this thing. Send it back to hell."

"And if I don't?"

"You're up for a contract renegotiation soon, right?"

Her question was her answer.

Carla didn't care about defeating a demon. She didn't care what happened to Chelsea Hopper or me. All she wanted was the ratings.

Ambrosia waved at me frantically, begging me to come to her, to get in front of the camera. "Five, four, three . . ."

I took one quick peek at Chelsea, and then I realized that I desperately wanted her to keep that smile. I hated to admit it, but Carla was right. We needed to defeat that thing and send it back to the darkness so Chelsea could live her life in sunshine.

I darted over to the walkway and hopped in front of the camera just as the live feed opened, clasping my hands together, fingers intertwined, giving the audience my signature bow.

"Welcome, friends, families, and to the millions of you watching around the world. This is simply unbelievable." I had to strain to keep the fake smile going. "We have the most incredible show you'll ever see on this very special, live Halloween episode of *Graveyard: Classified*. We asked for it, you delivered. After watching the ghastly evidence the Hoppers collected on their own, choking back tears during their desperate pleas for help, hundreds of thousands of votes were cast online, and you picked the winner. Let me introduce you to the Most Haunted House in America."

The "Most Haunted House in America" might have been a misnomer, because we had no way to confirm that, but damn, it sounded good. For all we knew, the house down the street from your grandmother might have been as scary as a spare bedroom in hell. The age-old adage for news is, "If it bleeds, it leads." In the world of paranormal reality shows, we said, "If it *screams*, it leads."

I stepped sideways, sweeping my hand back and up the walkway in the direction of the Hoppers' former home.

I felt like that was a rather anticlimactic speech, because it totally wasn't what I was prepared to say. I had something deeper, stronger, more powerful and cogent written and ready to go. My indecision cost me, because I lost every damn memorized word of it and had to concoct that bland nonsense on the fly.

Moving completely out of the way, I allowed the first camera to race up the cobblestone path to the front door, and as per the production plan, the live feed switched to a prerecorded segment. It cut to an interior tour of the house, with my voiceover in the background, as I narrated the inconceivable terrors that the Hoppers had endured while living there.

It really was a quiet, unassuming house, sort of a faded pistachio color with off-white shutters, a wraparound porch, and a front door painted soft beige. Two stories tall, with a tiny attic—where the demon lived—and colorful landscaping, the house possessed a heart blacker than coal. If houses have auras, and some of my psychic acquaintances insist they do, then that one seethed with the absence of light.

I knew that the intro piece—the tour of the home and my voiceover work—would last two minutes and seventeen seconds exactly. I used this time to dash over to the Hoppers who were standing patiently, though they looked nervous behind false grins, a pathetic attempt at convincing themselves that everything would be okay.

"You're sure about this?" I asked. "Last chance to back out."

Deep down, the part of my brain that governed *rational* thinking wanted them to. The *emotional* side was saying, "Let's go for it. I can make this better for you," and, also, "The ratings! Holy freakin' cow, the ratings!"

Rob Hopper said, "We just want it to be over, Mr. Ford."

"We trust you," Leila added. "We know you won't let anything happen to her."

I leaned down and took Chelsea's soft, sticky hands. She had a ring of chocolate around her lips. Her sweet breath smelled like peppermint candy. "Chelsea, you ready to go beat up a ghost?"

She giggled, put her chin down to her shoulder and twisted bashfully from side to side. "Uh-huh. But will it be scary?"

"Maybe a little. I'll protect you, though. If we go in there and kick this thing's hiney, all those bad dreams might go away. Does that sound like a plan?"

Chelsea scrunched up her nose. "You said 'hiney.'"

"I did, didn't I?"

Over my shoulder, I heard Ambrosia softly calling my name. "Mr. Ford? Mr. Ford? Thirty seconds. Intro's almost finished."

I stood and said to the Hoppers, "I'll protect her. It'll be fine, I promise."

Was I lying? The scary thing was, I didn't know the answer to that.

"Listen to the crew. They'll give you directions and timing. We're live for three hours tonight, but Chelsea will come in after thirty minutes—anyway, yeah. You're in good hands with these guys."

I retreated a step, ready to jog up to my next mark on the front porch, and Chelsea brought me to a heartbreaking halt when she said, "Don't let the dark man get me, okay?"

# CHAPTER 5

Detective Thomas has to sit down before he says, "It was a black mass about five feet tall, looked almost like it was flowing. Malleable, you know? Swirling around itself. It was standing there in the doorway, watching me. I took a couple of steps back, and—and I blinked really hard, kinda rubbed my eyes, thinking maybe it was just a trick of the light, but then I thought, can't be, I've already been inside for thirty minutes. You know how your eyes are sorta messed up when you look at the sun, like maybe out the window or whatever? You get those blobs in your vision? It was like that, but . . . real." He points toward the living room entryway and the hall beyond. "The thing was solid. I couldn't see past it. And I remember it as clear as day, I said, 'What the—' and before I could finish my sentence, I swear to God, I swear on the life of my poor mother, may she rest in peace, it was like this thing opened its eyes. Two red, glowing orbs revealed themselves slowly. I coulda screamed, Mr. Ford. I coulda called out to God but I was so . . . cold on the inside. Like looking at this thing froze my heart. All my happiness that I'd ever had, just *poof*, gone."

His last words come out in a whisper as he holds an empty hand over his chest, clawlike, and squeezes the air.

He adds, "In all those shows you've done, you ever seen anything like that?"

"I have in person, absolutely," I answer. "Though we were never able to catch it on film. I believe there's a variety of shadow people out there, Detective Thomas, some with less power who show up as something like a floating mass or like a misty cloud up in the corner of a room. Then you have the ones that're strong enough to appear in physical form, like being able to make out a head and shoulders, maybe even arms. I've seen those plenty of times with my own eyes, standing right there in the same room with them. I've been able to capture those on film, both with digital cameras and video recorders, plenty of evidence that those exist. But what you're talking about, the ones with the red eyes? They're too strong, too powerful, too . . . intelligent to get caught."

Detective Thomas scoffs and leans forward in the chair. "You're telling me that thing has a brain?"

"Well, there are two different types of haunts, detective. Residual and intelligent. Residual hauntings are like, say, leftover energy. Think of a tape recorder that's stuck in an infinite loop. If you're in a haunted house and you hear the same footsteps climbing the staircase every night at a quarter past twelve, that's a residual haunt. That tape recorder is simply resetting itself and playing again."

"So the ghost doesn't know it's doing it? It's totally unaware that it's stuck in limbo, repeating itself throughout eternity?"

"More or less."

"Sounds like my ex-wife." He chuckles at his own joke, and I offer a sympathy laugh. Craghorn sits patiently and quietly on the sofa, hands in his lap. His eyes keep flicking up, and his gaze lingers on something behind me. There's another entrance back there, which leads into the kitchen, and I feel a sensation of eyes on the back of my neck. A quick glance reveals nothing, and when I turn back around, Craghorn is again focused on his fingernails. The pace of his breathing has increased, but he's otherwise normal.

And, of course, I use the term "normal" loosely.

I tell Detective Thomas, "The other type of haunting is what we call an 'intelligent' haunt, and that's where the person or thing is self-aware enough to respond to questions or communicate outright. Like if I'm using a digital recorder and I ask, 'What's your name?' and upon review, I hear a response that says, 'Steve Pendragon.' And with all the research I've prepared beforehand, I know that a Steve Pendragon used to live in the location, then that's an intelligent haunt."

Without looking up, Craghorn mumbles quietly, "Episode three-oh-seven. Fort Lauderdale, October 2005."

"Wow, yeah. Exactly." It surprises me to hear that Craghorn knows the show so well.

Detective Thomas stands up and paces back and forth in front of the fireplace. "Sorry, I feel safer on my feet. So you said that a person or *thing* can be self-aware enough to communicate. What'd you mean by *thing?*"

I catch Craghorn looking over my shoulder again. Like a quarterback telegraphing a pass, his eyes follow something from left to right.

I have to look, too. I can't *not* look.

Again, there's nothing there, but damn if he's not freaking me out. I answer, "I could give you an entire history of the paranormal world, detective, from demons to subdemons, to angels, to sprites, to fairies, whatever, but my guess is, you'd only like to know what in the hell it was that you saw, right?"

He crosses his arms and waits.

"Dark, full-bodied being, clearly humanoid in shape and size, glowing red eyes? That's a top-tier demon, detective. What you saw, he's not riding the pine on any of Satan's teams; he's out on the infield playing. Front lines. The starting first baseman."

Detective Thomas snorts and shakes his head. "You're telling me I saw a *demon?*"

If he hadn't seen what he'd seen, right about now is the spot where he'd tell me that I'm a charlatan, that I'm a snake-oil salesman, and that I'm making all of this up for ratings in order to give people a thrill.

That's the thing, see—when it comes to ghosts, aliens, demons, or, hell, even Sasquatch and the Loch Ness Monster, it's easy to be a skeptic until you've actually witnessed it.

On one hand, I feel bad for the nonbelievers because they're missing out on so much. If they'd only open their minds, there's another world out there, so much more life to experience than breakfast cereal, sitcoms, and a comfortable recliner.

On the other, I feel even worse for the witnesses who are far fewer in number. They're the minority. Some have seen, and they know, and yet they hide, because they're afraid of the ridicule. They're afraid of losing their jobs or having their communities label them a freak or a weirdo.

Man, I get that. I've been there my whole life. It's not easy being an outcast. At least not until you head up the number-one paranormal show on the planet.

Then there are the brave souls who are willing to come forward and testify under the penalty of ridicule that they saw something. That's courage right there.

Detective Thomas is in this latter category, simply by calling me in, bringing me here, and telling this story, but he hasn't quite accepted that he saw what he saw.

Maybe it was my fault, his sarcastic snort just now. If I'd told him, yeah, that was nothing more than a plain-old, garden-variety ghost, he might have accepted it and moved on. However, by explaining that he witnessed something far worse, something made up of the blackest evil, a top-tier demon on Satan's council, well, I'm pretty sure I just blew his mind.

That's confirmed when he says, "I really don't know what to say to that, Mr. Ford. A demon. A demon?" He keeps repeating the word in various states of inflection, as if finding the proper way to get it out would make it more acceptable. It's only two syllables, yeah, but it's kind of amazing how many different ways he's able to pronounce it.

After roughly the eighth iteration, when he can't possibly squeeze any more inflection out of those two straightforward syllables that hold so much weight, apparently Craghorn can't take it anymore. He slings his hands up over his ears and screams, "Enough, enough, enough!" and stomps his feet on the ground like a child throwing a tantrum.

Detective Thomas freezes and turns to him. "Hey, now, ease up. I'm just trying to wrap my mind around—"

"Not you, idiot," Craghorn hisses angrily. "*He* won't shut up."

The temperature of the room drops another five degrees. I stand up and immediately turn around, searching the kitchen behind me where Craghorn's eyes had focused on something earlier. It's empty. I understand whom he means, but Detective Thomas is confused. "Who, Craghorn? Who won't shut up?"

Craghorn says in a childlike voice, "Him. There," and points.

I don't see anything. Neither does the detective because he asks, "Who are you talking about? It's just the three of us."

"No. You're wrong. Dead wrong."

I back up a step. Whatever Craghorn was pointing at is in my vicinity, and if we're definitely dealing with a "Tier One" in this house, like the filth that inhabited the Hopper home, then I should probably keep my distance. I'm not prepared for this, not in the slightest. I expected to come in here and have Detective Thomas tell me that he saw the ghost of Louisa Craghorn. I expected he'd tell me about a full-bodied apparition and that I'd do a couple of EVP sessions, ask Louisa who murdered her, and, I hope, dig up another clue for Thomas to go on.

Naively, I assumed that this would be a fairly quick one-and-done kind of moment.

There's no wonder the detective was so hesitant to explain himself back at the station.

Craghorn says, "No, damn you. I will not."

"Dave," I say gently, trying to reach out to him. "Is it the demon? Do you see it?"

"He's here. He's with us now."

Detective Thomas whips his head left and right, looking for it. He retreats to a rocking chair in the corner, close to the light of the windows, and yanks his sidearm out of his shoulder holster. Even with the barrel aimed at the ceiling, I don't want this guy to get spooked and fire off a round, possibly hitting one of us in the process.

I tell him to put it away, that a bullet isn't going to stop this thing no matter what. The fact that his weapon, his shield, his security blanket, isn't going to stop what's in the room with us sends his bottom lip to quivering.

Nearly blubbering, he says, "Make it go away, Ford. You know how these things operate, right? Get it out of here."

"I wish it was that easy."

Craghorn is standing beside me now, whimpering and whining. The sounds coming out of his mouth aren't words—at least not English ones—and it takes me a moment to realize that he may be muttering in an ancient language, powerful words that died thousands of years ago. I've heard it before, but only a few times, and only in the presence of something like this.

Craghorn also attempts a pathetic escape. He stumbles and falls back onto the couch, trying to shove himself deeper and deeper into the cushions, pushing farther away from this invisible entity that's stalking him.

I can't believe that something this mighty hasn't manifested yet. Perhaps it's using the available energy to communicate with Craghorn.

Every inch of my skin prickles, and I feel the humming, vibrating sensation coursing through me. I feel weakened, as if it's stealing my energy. I'm dizzy, exhausted, like I haven't slept in days. My chest is heavy. I have an emotional anvil sitting on my heart.

"Ford?" Detective Thomas tries to get my attention. "What's going on? You okay?"

I've been in this situation before, hundreds of times, and normally I can handle this.

But when it rolls past, I know I've never encountered something as . . . as *strong* as this. Like a wave slinking toward the shore, the pressure, the sensation of death pushes by me.

Craghorn shoves his body away with a foot planted firmly on the hardwood floor, the other leg pathetically moving up and down, trying to gain a foothold and failing. He arches his back and turns his head sideways, whimpering, "No. No, please. Don't."

And then I watch as a handful of his shoulder-length hair is lifted and his head yanked to the side, pulling him from one side of the couch to the other.

I am goddamn terrified. Why? The smallest explanations often carry the most weight.

This is bad.

Very, very bad.

# CHAPTER 6

Mike Long is like a brother to me. Or he was until the night I went through with exposing Chelsea Hopper to that thing in the attic.

We built *Graveyard: Classified* up from a few piddling online videos years ago to the international powerhouse that it was before the network ripped it from primetime. We met in a junior-college film class, bonding over horror movies and the mutual adrenaline rush we got when we were trying to film our own in places where we didn't have permission. The night we sneaked into an abandoned mental hospital with six cheerleaders who were half-naked and drunk, was the last night we would ever work from a poorly written script.

When we captured that full-bodied apparition, a woman in a white nightgown, who seemed to be pleading with us to help her, that's all we needed to go back again and again, giving up on fictional stories and trying to capture real ones on camera.

We never saw her after that night. Perhaps it was enough for her to know that someone had received her message, and she passed blissfully on to the next phase of the afterlife. We, too, moved on to other decaying insane asylums and old factories, homes, churches, antique shops, and lighthouses. Anywhere that was supposedly haunted, we would ask permission and perform an investigation, then upload our videos online. Hundreds of thousands of followers would flock to them, and it wasn't long before a group of producers from The Paranormal Channel came calling, offering better equipment, an actual film crew, and contracts that promised more money than we had ever thought possible from a weekend hobby.

Mike and I, we were inseparable. He was my best man when I married Melanie from wardrobe. He made David Letterman and Ellen laugh. He was the straight man to my crazy, gung-ho attitude when it came to paranormal investigations.

We've only spoken once since the show was cancelled. His end of the conversation consisted of three words: "Go to hell."

If he sees my number on the caller ID, he might not pick up.

But, Jesus, I hope he does. After what I saw inside the Craghorn place, I don't just *want* his help, I *need* it. There's no one else in the world that I would trust with this level of evil.

Outside the house, it's 104 degrees here on the sidewalk, but I'm shivering. Detective Thomas paces back and forth, snorting like a dragon, mumbling empty, macho threats about going back inside because he never backs down from a fight. I notice he's not in a hurry to go back up the stairs.

Dave Craghorn sits on the bottom step, hunched over, cradling himself. There's a small patch of hair missing on the side of his head. I can see it from here.

My hand instinctively goes up to the back of my neck when I feel a burning sensation, but then I realize it's just the sun beating down. There's no demon out here clawing me. That's how it usually starts, though, with the scratches. You feel like a patch of your skin is on fire, it'll take on a subtle pink hue like it's a superficial burn, then the marks will gradually show up. I've had angry spirits claw me more times than I care to recall, but I've never seen anything powerful enough to rip the hair right out of someone's head.

Well, that's not necessarily true. I can think of one other that was just as strong.

Two years ago. A faded pistachio house in Cleveland.

I stare at my phone, Mike's number is sitting there on the screen, almost as if it's pulsing, throbbing, alive and waiting on me to take the chance. I have to; Mike needs to see this. I press "Send" and hold the cell up to my ear, air caught in my lungs.

A warm breeze whips through the space between the homes to my right, pushes my hair to the side, yet offers no relief. With the temperature and humidity combined, it feels like a steaming column erupting from a kettle.

The phone rings and rings.

Detective Thomas paces. Craghorn hugs himself and rocks, muttering unintelligible words.

Finally, a voice on the other end of the line snarls, "What in the hell do you want?"

"Mike. Holy shit, thanks for picking up."

"I'm not interested, whatever it is."

"Wait. *Wait.* Don't hang up."

"In fact, I'm not even sure why I answered."

I don't believe this, not entirely. He saw my number. He could've dismissed it, deleted my inevitable voice mail sight unseen. No, he saw that it was me, and he knows I'd only call for something serious. The fact that he answered means there's a tiny bit of Mike that may have forgiven me. It's a start, at least.

"I need help, dude. I'm up against something righteous here. It's powerful. I could really use you."

He tries to stifle a laugh. "You're shitting me, right? Are you still flying around the country, feeding bullshit to whoever will listen to you? Who is it this time? Some backwoods, trailer-park sheriff in the middle of nowhere? That's what you're doing, isn't it? Consulting with law enforcement? Anybody that wants to cut you a check to hear the great Ford Atticus Ford tell them lies?"

Mike is lashing out, obviously, because he knows that none of what I do now, and what we did for over ten years together, is built on lies. Now, and in the past, I operate on solid evidence, tangible things that can't be debunked. That was the one thing I would never compromise on when *Graveyard: Classified* aired; we absolutely would *not* allow content or evidence that could easily be debunked by tricks of the light, corrupted ambient noise, or anything of that sort. It had to be inexplicable and legitimate evidence before it would air. We tossed out thousands of hours of video and audio evidence—much to the chagrin of our producers—because we didn't want to risk our reputations.

When a certain young assistant producer, Carla's original understudy, suggested we fake evidence to liven up the show, he barely had the sentence out of his mouth before I was on the phone with the CEO of The Paranormal Channel. The guy was gone the next day.

Point is, Mike knows I don't make this shit up. I tell him, "I'm with a client, yes, here in Virginia Beach."

"And you didn't call when you got into town? I'm so disappointed." The sarcasm drips so thickly, he could douse an entire stack of flapjacks.

I accepted the job with Detective Thomas for several reasons. I was intrigued by the information he presented. I wanted to help with a case that was getting some national attention, because, if I really self-analyze, I'm looking for some of that old, familiar glory and a chance at redemption. Maybe there'll be another show in my future.

And, honestly, I was drawn to the Hampton Roads area because Mike's primary residence, one of his many multimillion dollar homes, is just over an hour and a half south, down in Kitty Hawk, North Carolina. It sits on about an acre of shoreline, making the tourists just as jealous as they are curious. They filmed a movie there back in the '90s, some romantic comedy starring—hell, I can't remember who, but the guy was about thirty years too old for the young lady.

The day Detective Thomas called, I heard the words, "Virginia Beach," and immediately thought, "Hey, that's close to Mike."

So it goes.

Mike says, "I figured those big city boys would think twice about tarnishing their badges with the likes of—"

"Enough, okay? I get it. You hate me for ruining the show, you hate me for ignoring your advice, and you hate me for sending Chelsea into that attic. That's okay. That's fine. I can never apologize enough, and maybe I won't ever be able to redeem myself in your eyes, but let's put all that to the side for the moment. Please? I'm here in Portsmouth, and I've got a right-hander. Maybe the strongest one I've ever seen."

A "right-hander" is our slang for a Tier One demon that sits at the right hand of Satan. One of his go-to guys.

This grabs Mike's attention. He says, "Stronger than the Hopper house?"

"Possibly."

There's a hint of disbelief, along with a smile forming around his words as he says, "Wouldn't it be some shit if that thing was following *you*, and now it's, like, on steroids or something?"

"I . . . doubt that's the case."

The idea is both intriguing and frightening, and for a moment, I actually *do* entertain the thought. I've been through things that most people in the paranormal field haven't. Early on, mistakes were made. Mike and I both screwed up one too many times before we learned how to protect ourselves. We've been through minor possessions. Things followed us home. Our wives—Mike's current, my former—experienced too much, more than they deserved, in places that were supposed to be their private sanctuaries away from what Mike and I did publicly.

Then I remember . . . back at the old farmhouse, on the outskirts of Portland, the spirit had said Chelsea's name during the first investigation, and then the unbelievable things I caught when I was there with Ulie the other night.

I decide not to tell Mike about that yet. It'll cloud his judgment around whatever is going on here with Dave Craghorn, his house, his deceased wife, and Detective Thomas's investigation. And that's if I can talk him into helping.

I tell Mike, "Can't be. The right-hander in this house was here before they called me in. The detective I'm working with, and the homeowner, both of them, have seen a shadow figure in the past. Humanoid, about five feet tall, with glowing red eyes. That's why I'm here. This poor guy, Craghorn, he's living here all by himself and, no lie, during the interview earlier, I'm standing there in the living room with him and the detective. Neither of us can see what's going on, but Craghorn starts trying to get away from this thing—it never did manifest, but it creeps up on the guy and boom, his hair gets yanked hard enough to toss him like a dishtowel. Whole clump of it came right out of his head. Swear to God."

What Mike hears, out of all that, is this: "Did I hear you right? Did you say Craghorn?"

"Yeah. Why?"

"Oh God, Ford, you're not chasing the ambulances now, are you? That's the case with the mayor and the dead secretary? Showed up on the news again about six months ago?"

I exhale, feeling the thick, humid air escaping my lungs, then reach up and wipe a sopping layer of sweat off my forehead. "That's the one."

"And what angle are you working? Hoping to get the show back with a high profile case?"

"No, but it can't hurt." I hate to admit it openly, but there's no use in trying to hide my submotivations from Mike. He knows me too well.

"Ford, this is ridiculous."

"What happens in the future has no bearing on what's happening right now. This poor guy . . . Mike, he seriously needs our help. He needs some peace. From what I can see, he seems like he could be normal, but he also looks like an emaciated meth head just by trying to exist in his own home. I have no idea how a right-hander ties in with Craghorn's murdered wife, but I promised the detective I'd do whatever I could to help him with any possible leads.

"If this thing has been here all along, maybe it wasn't a murder. Maybe she *was* having an affair, the demon got into her head, and she threw herself off a bridge. Detective Thomas told me that her body showed signs of choking, but what if this thing got into her mind? We've seen it before—people trying to gouge out their own eyes, trying to choke themselves to death. Remember that one lady who tried to pull out her own tongue with a set of pliers? I need to get back in there. I need to ask it some questions, and I sure as hell would feel a lot better about doing it if you were here. And it doesn't have to be for me. Help the detective. Help Craghorn. That's what we used to be all about, right? At least back in the day? Whether they were alive or dead, we are always trying to give somebody *peace*."

There's a long spate of silence on the other end. For a moment, I think he might have hung up on me, and I delivered my best speech to dead air.

I'm about to ask if he's still on the line when I hear a resigned, "Text me the address. I'll be there in a couple of hours."

# CHAPTER 7

Mike arrives.

I meet him up the street, about half a block from the Craghorn place. Detective Thomas and Dave hang back, staring at the front door with wary glances, as if they're waiting on something to step outside and slither down the stairs.

Mike is dressed in his usual attire of khaki shorts, a T-shirt, and flip-flops. He used to be one of those heavier guys who wore shorts no matter what time of year it was, whether we were in the upper reaches of North Dakota in the middle of January, investigating a haunted ranch, or if we were down in Key West hunting Hemingway's ghost.

*Used* to be. I haven't seen him in two years—he was never much for Facebook or Twitter back when the show was on, choosing to keep his private life to himself—so I've missed out on the fact that he seems to have lost close to a hundred pounds. Seriously. I barely recognize the dude.

He looks healthy. Tanned. The sleeves of his T-shirt are straining against his biceps, and now, rather than stretching tight around a spare tire, the soft cotton pulls against his pecs.

"Mike," I say, unable to contain a smile, "look at you, man. You're—damn, I bet Toni *loves* this, huh?" I offer my hand to shake.

59

He ignores my compliment, and my hand, as he gives me one of two pelican cases, these large, black boxes that are like suitcases on steroids. They come with an interior made of forgiving foam for cushions, and over the years, they saved our sensitive equipment more times than Jesus saved souls. "Here, take this," he says, continuing his purposeful march down the sidewalk, flip-flops slapping sharply against his heels. Glancing back, he scrutinizes me and says, "Seems like we're going in opposite directions, chief. Put on a pound or twelve, huh? And what's that shit in your hair? It looks like somebody dipped a porcupine in black lard."

"Leave the gel out of this. I'm trying something new. Besides, I'm still better looking, no matter how many pounds you dropped."

"If you're desperate enough to base your confidence on the word of thirteen-year-old girls, don't let me stop you." He's not smiling. I don't think he's joking. "Anyway, I came to work. Somebody else can stroke your ego."

What I thought was a nice start, with cajoling and good-natured ribbing, might actually be Mike sniping at me, which I should've expected. I change the subject, hoping that by talking shop, he might lighten up. "You brought your own equipment?" I try to match his pace.

"Why wouldn't I? You never came prepared before, and I doubt you've changed much."

Mike's right, sort of, and I humbly admit it. "Preparation, probably not, but mentally, I'm nowhere near where I was two years ago. I can promise you that. Chelsea changed me."

"She changed your paycheck." A car honks down at the end of the block, like it's an exclamation mark at the end of his sentence.

"Come on now, that's not fair—"

"Ford, save it. I'm not here for you or to have that discussion again. I'm here to keep you from screwing up somebody else's life with another right-hander, got it?"

"I—fine." He knows I'm just as qualified as he is, even if I was unprepared with the technical stuff on occasion, but I was as equally adept at investigating—if not better— at least when it came to tapping into the emotional side of spirits and hauntings. This vitriol, it's about punishing me, and until he gets it out of his system, there's no use in trying to fight it or convince him otherwise.

When I was a kid, my grandmother used to tell me this old wives' tale about how if a snapping turtle latched on to you, it wouldn't let go until the sky thundered. That's how Mike is when he gets an idea into his head.

I think that maybe if we can get into the groove of an investigation, just like old times, he might soften a bit, and then I can have a real conversation with him.

We reach the detective and Craghorn, making quick work of the introductions. Mike is all business with the detective and soft and reassuring with the diminutive man who's been beaten down in his own home. Craghorn barely meets Mike's eyes, then he resumes the unrelenting study of his shoes.

Mike says to Detective Thomas, "Can you tell me what happened?"

"You mean now, or before?"

61

I start to explain, and Mike flashes me an annoyed look, holding up his palm. "I asked *him*."

"Okay. Whatever." I'd like to keep the peace here, so shutting up seems to be the best approach.

Mike listens intently as Detective Thomas goes through his story again, starting at the beginning with the original investigation as he did with me back at his desk. I've heard all of this already, and it's fresh in my mind, so I tune out their discussion. I should be paying attention. I should be listening for any more clues that I may not have picked up on earlier, but I can't help it. I'm gone, thinking about the glory days when Mike and I, and the rest of the gang, would arrive at a location and do our initial interviews with our clients.

There was always this excited hum in the air as the crew set up their equipment and we listened to the clients' stories, took notes, and crossed our fingers that, yeah, we could give them some closure, some answers, but at the same time, we were always hoping for another Holy Grail moment. Another full-bodied apparition caught on camera or a levitating dinner plate, something that couldn't be explained away by the doubters who accused us of trickery and crafty video editing.

It's hard to explain what an investigation is really like until you've done one, or several hundred, or a thousand.

Often, there's a lot of waiting, a lot of silence, a lot of waking Mike up at three in the morning when he's snoozing on a forgotten mattress. A lot of crossing your fingers that something will present itself. Sometimes it does, sometimes it doesn't. Just because a spirit doesn't provide some sort of evidence on the random Tuesday and Wednesday you're there investigating doesn't mean the place isn't haunted; it just means that the spirit world wasn't highly active that day.

Back when the show was chugging along and we were doing twenty-two episodes per season, there was a lot of down time while the crew set up and scouted angles. Mics were checked. Cameras and recorders had batteries replaced.

Oh, man, the batteries. Batteries upon batteries. We probably kept Duracell in business on our own.

With or without *Graveyard: Classified*, every investigation I've been on is a coin flip that's governed by chance, luck, and timing; life and the afterlife are bonded by those three things.

But when it all works out, and the investigation is a winner?

I'll take an espresso and two shots of adrenaline to go, please. Sign me up.

Things that go bump in the night have terrified people since we had to look out for nocturnal predators, praying that our campfires didn't burn out. No matter how many times you've flipped off the last switch and encased yourself in darkness, daring or begging something to show itself, there are times when you'll get spooked.

You'll hold your breath and feel every square inch of skin prickle. You'll want to scream. You'll want to run, but damn it, you have to fight that flight instinct because there's something out there, something from the other side, and it's dragging a sharp fingernail down a window, or some

Civil War soldier is pleading for you to get a message to his children, or a shamed servant is apologizing for taking her own life. A piano plays by itself in another room. Footsteps echo across the wooden floor overhead when you *know* you're alone.

I've seen and heard so much. I've never faked even the tiniest of things, like a piece of dust on a camera lens. What do the hip kids say these days? Haters gonna hate, right?

Well, doubters gonna doubt.

As I daydream about past investigations, the good ol' days, my eyes drift around the neighborhood, inspecting the nearby homes.

Like I said, I normally don't pause to appreciate this stuff, but since Detective Thomas seems to be retelling his story starting with the book of Genesis, I have a couple of minutes. *In the beginning, God created demons and shitheels. . .*

Despite my typical reservations, the architecture here actually *is* pretty fantastic with a lot of stones and crenellations, high windows, and pure craftsmanship displayed in the front doors. These homes were built back when people took pride in their hard work. It's nothing like the homes in my neighborhood that are governed by a snippy HOA board: mow your grass to a quarter of an inch below standard; you have too many dandelions; you're not allowed to have a gnome in your flowerbed.

I swear an entire house popped up in a week around the corner from me. One day it was an empty lot, I left for an investigative trip to Lansing, Michigan, and when I got back, *boom*, house.

Anyway, if you didn't know what lurked inside his walls, Craghorn's place is beautiful and does the neighborhood justice. Minus the dying flowers and shrubs that haven't been tended to in God knows how long, minus the powerful demon controlling the interior, I'd love to call this place home.

"Ford!"

"Hmm?" I mumble, daydream interrupted.

Mike asks, "Did you see that?"

I clear my throat and cross my arms, making a decent attempt at looking like I was paying attention. "Yeah, it was up there, and, uh . . ."

"Second floor window. The curtain dropped back like somebody pulled away."

For the first time in an hour . . . no, longer, since he was attacked and we retreated to the safety of the sidewalk, Craghorn speaks a coherent sentence. He says, "That's where it likes to stay."

"It?" Mike asks. "You mean the . . ."

"Yeah. Him."

There's a layer of sharp acrimony in Craghorn's voice that I'm hearing for the first time. Perhaps he's recovering from earlier. Perhaps he feels emboldened now that the paranormal defense team is fully present.

"That was my wife's study. She used to paint in there." Craghorn clenches his jaw, the muscle rising and falling underneath loose skin. His mouth purses, his nose scrunches as he glares up at the window. I halfway expect him to make a fist and shake it like some old codger.

Mike is about to ask another question when Detective Thomas excuses himself and takes a phone call. We wait patiently while he listens to his caller, lifting his shoulders in a sorry-can't-help-it apology. Finally, he hangs up and tells us he has to go. "Wife was reminding me about my visit to the doc. Checking out the ticker today," he says, patting his chest. "After what happened in there, I feel like I should keep the appointment. Tell you what, Mr. Craghorn is in good hands here. You know what you're doing, and I'm pretty sure I'm not going back inside that goddamn place ever again. So, you do what you do, and then come meet me back at the station. That work for you guys?"

Craghorn's gaze flitters upward, looking as if he's slightly worried that the man with the gun is leaving, and I don't bother telling him that bullets would only tickle that thing inside his house.

I say to Detective Thomas, "We've got it all under control," then toss another subtle compliment at Mike. "He's the best at what he does, so if we're able to find anything for you, it'll be because he's here."

You catch more bees with honey.

The detective gives us a cordial salute and spins on his heels. He's down the sidewalk, around the corner with his step looking lighter, and gone before anyone else speaks again.

Craghorn is the first to say something. "Good thing for him."

"Why's that?" Mike asks.

"I can't repeat what the dark man inside said about the detective."

My lungs clench, and Mike flashes me a worried glance.

Maybe it's just coincidence—could be nothing at all—but it's so odd that he refers to it using the same words as Chelsea Hopper.

*"Don't let the dark man get me, okay?"*

I can see tremors of the past rippling across Mike's face. At first, I think he's reliving the moment with that little blonde angel bobbing down the hallway, excited to help and so thrilled to be with her new friends from TV. A thousand pounds of regret fill my stomach. I'm aching and anxious to get back to fighting for her retribution.

I think Mike is going to sympathize with me. He's going to tell Dave Craghorn that it'll be okay. We've fought things like this before, and we're going to get his life back. We're going to give his wife the everlasting rest she deserves.

I think this, and I'm about to say something to Craghorn, but Mike's fist connects with my jaw, and I drop like my chute didn't open. I blink, trying to see around the sparkles dancing in my vision.

Before I can clear my head, there are rough hands on my shirt, yanking me up. Mike says, "You put him up to this, didn't you? The dark man? Really, Ford? Did you think I'd come running back for that?"

I taste blood. I try to tell him no, that I never said a word to Craghorn about Chelsea or the dark man, but I'm dizzy and confused.

My words come out jumbled. I can make out the red hue in Mike's skin, the rage twisting his features, and then his forehead meets the bridge of my nose.

I succumb to the darkness.

# CHAPTER 8

I come to, and it takes me a second to realize that a few minutes have passed. I've been moved, and instead of lying on the searing sidewalk outside, knocked unconscious, I'm stretched out on Craghorn's couch. It's freezing in here.

I quickly sit up. A spark of fear shoots throughout my body—I'm inside, alone, where the dark man is—and then my eyesight swims just enough to send me back down, hand on my forehead and groaning. The coppery hint of blood remains on my tongue and I feel the dried, caked aftereffects of Mike's headbutt on my upper lip. My eyelids and nose are slightly puffy, and the bulge hinders my vision. When I drop my left arm, I feel an ice pack resting against my thigh.

At least they were a little considerate, and I hold the ice up to my face, wincing and hissing with the pain.

I wonder where Mike and Craghorn are, and it occurs to me that Mike might have been pissed enough to drop me off inside, alone, as a tasty, immobile sacrifice to whatever abomination inhabits this house. If that's the case, I picture myself tied to a railroad track with a locomotive bearing down on me, horn wailing, but there's no cowboy in sight coming to my rescue. There's no flying man in a cape, swooping down to sweep me away. No fireman with a ladder or a helicopter pilot with a dangling harness. You know, standard hero shit.

My mind does that sometimes, goes places. If you've spent enough time in silence, as I have, waiting on a sign from the afterlife or something to manifest, it's easy for your imagination to run unchecked. I should write books. I bet I could give Carter Kane a run for his money.

While I'm pondering my demise and picturing the dark man bearing down upon me, I hear voices in the distance, maybe down the hallway and upstairs, and I realize that it's Mike and Craghorn.

Thank God they haven't left me in here entirely alone.

It sounds like an informative discussion, but mostly it's Mike asking questions and Craghorn responding. He's such a hushed and beaten-down man, I can barely hear his replies.

Mike says, "That happened in here?" And seconds later, he follows up with, "That was only six months ago? When Detective Thomas came back? Interesting."

I make a concentrated effort to sit up, but slowly and cautiously, to give my throbbing face and woozy head a chance to catch up. One last groan, and I push myself to my feet.

You'd think I'd be used to things like this now, but there's a large mirror above the fireplace, and a peek at my own reflection spooks me. I chuckle at how ridiculous this is—the great and mighty ghost hunter scared of himself—but I wasn't expecting it to be there. Mike would probably say it's an improvement, because I really do look like Wile E. Coyote hit me in the face with a fat hammer from Acme. Blood is caked in tendrils around my mouth and crawls down my neck. Luckily I'm wearing a black T-shirt, my trademark, so you can't tell how thoroughly it's soaked, which is enough for it to pull against my skin when I turn away from the mirror. It's the same sensation you get when you pull a scab off too early.

*\*\**

I find them in the upstairs hallway. Craghorn is in his submissive stance, hands clasped at his belt buckle, hunched over like he's waiting to be reprimanded, examining his shoelaces.

At first, I think Mike is simply standing with his arms crossed as he surveys the photographs hanging on the walls, but upon closer inspection, I see that he's trying to warm himself. If the downstairs was cold, this is igloo territory up here. He sees me coming, drops his hands to his waist, and shakes his head. He tries to say something, but it comes out halting, like trying to start a car on a freezing day.

"It's okay," I tell him. "I probably deserved that."

Mike clears his throat. "Right," he says, then adds, "I'll buy you a beer later."

"Make it a steak and we're even."

He lifts a corner of his mouth in a genuine attempt at a smile. The steak thing, that's a running joke going back a few years, before the show was a hit, back when we were starving college students who would trade the promise of a high-dollar steak on bets and dares while we stole handfuls of coffee creamer from a convenience store just to have milk for cereal.

That's old history between us, and it's gratifying to see that he can't headbutt good memories in the face.

"You should call that detective," Mike says. He lifts a digital voice recorder and waggles it. "We need to do a full investigation. Not just an afternoon asking questions. There's no way we can properly comb this place and then meet him back at the office this evening with some answers."

I nod toward the recorder. "You catch something?"

"Class A. It's a strong one." Mike stares down at the display, breathing heavily through his nose, as he rewinds the recording to the proper timestamp.

"You think it's . . ." My words trail off.

Mike doesn't need me to finish my sentence. He knows. "Do I think it's the right-hander from the Hopper place?" He pinches his lips together, tilts his head from side to side, lifting his shoulders. "What're the odds, you know? I don't think it is. Tone is off, but then again, I was just explaining to Mr. Craghorn about how demonic entities can mimic other spirits, other animals. You know the drill. Anyway . . . honestly, I think the fact that he called it 'the dark man' was a one-in-a-million coincidence. Bad timing, whatever, and, unluckily for you, it was just the right set of words to light a fuse that I wanted lit for two years."

I chuckle. "If that's a disguised apology, I accept. What'd you catch?"

"Two voices, actually, and Mr. Craghorn, if you don't want to hear this again, it's fine if you step away."

Craghorn slowly lifts his head. "I'll be downstairs."

Mike waits until Craghorn is gone, head disappearing below the landing, footsteps whispering through the hallway, before he holds the digital voice recorder up and plays the audio file.

There's silence, followed by Mike's flip-flops slapping against his heels, and then comes the sound of a doorknob. The creaking hinges groan like they're right off a Hollywood movie. Mike's voice says lightly, "Mark time at 5:38, that was Mr. Craghorn opening his bedroom door."

Paranormal investigators tag our own noises and manmade sounds, marking the location on our recordings, so when we go back to review our tapes for evidence we don't get our hopes up if we're the cause of something going bump in the night.

Mike's voice again, saying, "The energy in here is overwhelming. It's dark . . . a dark energy. Jesus, I could cry right now."

Which is followed by Craghorn mumbling, "Welcome to my life."

I hear the floorboards screech with the weight of a step, and Mike marks the time on that one as well. Now that I conduct investigations on my own, I'll typically let some standard sounds go, rather than tagging a sniffle or something like that every few minutes. I've done this enough to recognize that my own footsteps on a creaky floor don't need to be marked. It's second nature at this point, but I get the feeling that Mike is being overly cautious, or perhaps he's skittish about hopping back on the bicycle again after a long absence.

Mike, the actual one in the hallway with me, says, "Listen. The first EVP is right here." There's more silence, with a hint of moving air in the background, and I recognize that it's Mike's anxious breathing. Something has spooked him. "Did you see that?" his voice asks. "That ball of light in the corner?"

Mike points at the recorder. "Right here."

I lean down, turn my ear closer, and hear, "*I'm sorry, love.*"

"Wow," I whisper.

"Keep listening."

The same voice, a female's, says, "*Make it go.*"

"Make it go?" I repeat.

"Yeah. That's it for those. Let me fast forward. This one comes through five minutes later."

It sounds like they're still in the bedroom. Mike again mentions the dark, suffocating energy. He feels dizzy, as if there's a buzzing between his ears. Craghorn coughs. "You good?" Mike's voice asks.

"It feels like . . ." Craghorn answers. "Feels like something is squeezing my throat. I have to get . . ."

And then the rest of his words are mumbled, because a deep, guttural voice barrels in over top of Craghorn and says, "*Guilty . . . bitch . . . is mine.*"

It's so harsh, so evil, that the words feel like rusted razor blades carving my skin, and I recoil. I feel a wetness on my upper lip and realize that my nose has resumed its bloody waterfall. Part of me thinks that's natural.

Part of me thinks it isn't.

"You're bleeding again," Mike says, with more concern in his voice than I would expect from someone who recently smashed my nose with his forehead.

I wipe my upper lip and study my slick fingertips.

This is a warning.

\*\*\*

The three of us retreat to the front stoop. It's like climbing out of a freezer and stepping on the surface of the sun. The smell out here has changed. It's no longer that ever-present hint of coastal air. I think it's sulfur, or maybe it's my imagination. I could be projecting, feeling like it's trapped in my clothes. I'm trying awfully hard to convince myself that it's not, but the fact that Mike sniffs his T-shirt and grimaces·is proof enough.

Craghorn again confirms that the female voice belonged to his wife, Louisa.

He hasn't fully emerged from the black, impenetrable fog that seems to be hanging around him. However, he seems slightly more willing to converse now that he's heard her voice.

Mike gently peppers Craghorn with questions, trying to coax more information out of him, while I excuse myself to call Detective Thomas. Mike is a skilled interviewer when it comes to pruning information from a flustered client, while I work best with the dead.

I move down the sidewalk until I find an acceptable level of shade, out of the direct heat, and it occurs to me that we're in a situation where "hot as hell" and "cold as hell" are *both* true and relevant. It's hotter than hell out here, and Dave Craghorn has been living inside the cold hell of his house for months.

Detective Thomas answers on the third ring. "Yeah?" He sounds agitated, but then again, that appears to be his normal state of existence. "You find anything?"

I explain what Mike caught on the audio recorder—the female voice and the demonic one—repeating it word for word. Then I add, "It's bigger than what we thought. We'd like to do a full night investigation, and as a matter of fact, I recommend it."

"What? Why? You caught Craghorn's wife apologizing, and this thing saying she was guilty. That tells me that the infidelity, the thing with the diary, it's spot on, so I should definitely be focusing on that as a motive."

"Yeah, but motive for who?"

"Craghorn, the mayor, some hired hitman."

"I don't get the sense that Craghorn is your guy."

"All due respect, Mr. Ford, but you can leave the detective work to me."

I tell him I understand, though I hold my tongue, choking down what I want to say. I get this more often than I'd like. These police departments call me in to aid in an investigation because they're stumped, I'll tell them what I learned, and sometimes they get attitude if they feel like I'm upstaging their authority and skill sets.

Sometimes it's merely pride that gets in the way, and I get that, I really do. I wouldn't want anyone making a guest appearance on *Graveyard: Classified* and telling me all about how I was screwing up a paranormal investigation as much as a detective wouldn't want anyone telling him he'd been chasing the wrong tail on a murder case.

However, there are times when I have to push back. I live with enough darkness on my conscience. It needs a little light now and then.

"Give us one night," I say. "There's more here than that."

"Look, Ford, that little hint is enough. I got what I needed."

"One night. Sundown to sunup. That's all I'm asking. Give us twelve, eighteen hours, max. Noon tomorrow."

I listen to him grunt in resignation. "It won't be on my dime. I'm sitting here getting my ass chewed for bringing you on in the first place."

I check my watch. It's three minutes to five. "Pro bono from now on. We can get you more. I know we can."

"Fine," he says. "I doubt any of this will be admissible in court, but if you come away with something solid, it'll help."

"You won't regret it."

We hang up, and I stand there feeling good about this. It's cliché, I know, but I feel like the band is back together. Well, minus all the lights, cameras, crew, and a catered service cart with a giant bowl of M&Ms and finger sandwiches. Just Mike and me, back into the breach. Old days come 'round again. History repeats itself.

A jogger trudges past me, her ponytail limp in the heat and humidity, much like the rest of her. She's cute and trim, and like a gawking fool, I'm standing there admiring her physique when I manage to tear my eyes away from her fantastic calves long enough to notice she's wearing one of the original *Graveyard: Classified* T-shirts, back from the first season when we had that cheesy font that looked like the letters were made out of tombstones.

It's a blatant reminder of the days when things were going well.

A good omen.

Right?

# CHAPTER 9

## CHELSEA HOPPER
### TWO YEARS AGO
### A Very Special Live Halloween Episode

*"Enjoy Tiger Puffs, the cereal with bite!"*

The commercial ended with the large, orange cat giving a wink and a thumbs up. Off camera, Ambrosia the intern said, "You're on, Mr. Ford. Go live in four, three—"

In my head, I counted out *"Two, one,"* and then:

"Welcome back to those of you at home here in the US and the millions watching around the world. That's our one and only commercial break because we've just gotten word from our producers that we're absolutely shattering all sorts of viewership records tonight. The final numbers for our live *television* broadcast won't be in until later this week, but I can officially say that as of right now, we have over six point three *million* viewers tuned into our live-stream Internet broadcast on TheParanormalChannel.com. We can't thank our fans enough, and we certainly would not be where we are today without the Gravediggers. You're the best."

I walked down the hall of the Hopper house, my thick-soled boots clunking on the hardwood floors. The cameraman followed me, inching slowly forward.

"If you're just tuning in, we've been investigating the Hopper home, which you guys voted the Most Haunted House in America. So far, it's been wild. You heard those footsteps, you heard that faucet turn on by itself in the bathroom, and if you were paying attention, you probably noticed Mike's shirt being tugged when he was walking through the kitchen. Have another look."

A quick fifteen-second recap played on repeat three times, shown in the black-and-green light of our night-vision cameras. In the video, Mike walked across the linoleum floor, holding a digital voice recorder. He asked if the entity who made the footsteps, or turned on the faucet, would give him any further sign of his presence. Clear as could be, there was a visible tug on his collar, and it was strong enough to make Mike jump and accuse me of screwing with him, asking me why I did that, even though you could easily see that my hands were down at my sides.

It was such a great capture and we were positive that, indubitably, the doubters would be all over the Internet the next day proclaiming our heresy, trying to show how we could've pulled it off using filament line in an elaborate hoax. Whatever. It happened, *sans* shenanigans.

When the replay stopped and the cameras were on me once again, I'd taken a right turn into another hallway, where I now stood outside of little Chelsea Hopper's former bedroom. Directly above was a trap door that led to the attic, and Mike was stationed beside me with his hand on the dangling pull string. I could feel him seething, eyes boring into the side of my head. I wanted to tell him that it was too late, that he should just go with it and curse me afterward, and that I definitely regretted what we were about to do, but he should know better because we had a goddamn show to run with millions and millions of people watching.

"Ladies and gentlemen," I said, lowering my voice and pausing for dramatic effect, tenting my fingertips and holding them up to my lips, "what you're about to witness may not be suitable for young viewers."

It was tough. It really was.

Carla normally ran things from the production truck, but she was inside with us now, perhaps like a Roman emperor wanting to witness the gladiator carnage. She had this slightly psychotic, leering grin on her face, and for the briefest of moments, I thought about calling it off just to spite her.

But I didn't, because, holy shit, this was amazing television.

And I really, really *did* want to give Chelsea Hopper some tranquility in her life.

It was wrong, and I knew it, but both of those statements were true.

Ratings. Peace.

If Chelsea could beat that thing, if she could climb into the attic and face down her own personal demon and tell it to go to hell, she would come out a stronger person on the other side. That's what I was counting on.

Risky—so risky.

I paused too long, apparently, because over the cameraman's shoulder, Carla made a circular motion with her index finger, telling me to speed things up.

"Okay, here we go. You all know the story. Before our commercial break, we told you more about the Hoppers and the terror that reigned here during their time in this home. All the unimaginable horror, the torture they faced together while they tried to live their lives, but this entity in the attic," I said, angrily raising my voice, "what they called 'the dark man,' this *bastard* refused to let them live normally. We're here tonight to send this monster back to where it came from."

Carla nodded, touching the tip of her thumb and forefinger together, and if it was possible, her uncomfortable grin grew larger as she winked.

Behind me, and out of the camera's view, Mike whispered, "This is such bullshit."

I continued, "They say that the world corrupts innocence. We're all a fresh, clean canvas until life comes along and throws a smattering of paint on it like Jackson Pollock—just a crazy, wild, mishmash of experiences. That may be true, but what I like to believe is that innocence is a powerful weapon against evil. If evil has not yet corrupted a young mind, and if that young mind is given the power to face down malevolence and wickedness, then there is nothing more potent, nothing more capable of sending a demon back to hell."

I hardly believed a word of this, by the way, but it sounded pretty righteous.

However, strength, will, and determination *can* overcome the evil in our lives.

And really, what's more determined than a child who hasn't yet learned to compromise?

"This is why we're trying an unprecedented tactic this evening. You all know what trigger objects are, especially if you've seen the show more than once. Trigger objects—"

The bedroom door to my right slammed shut with enough force to shake the walls and rumble the floor underneath my feet. I yelped in fear. My skin prickled.

Mike shouted, "Dude!" and moved closer to me.

The cameraman, Don, scampered away and our audience got a shaky view for a moment. Don was a professional, however, and it only took him a second to recover. Also, off camera, I'm sure those watching clearly heard Carla exclaiming, "What the fuck was that?"

Or the bleeped version of it. We were broadcasting on a five-second delay from the live feed and those audio guys out in the van had speedy fingers.

The amount of paranormal energy it took to slam that door so hard was staggering. Right then, it became completely clear that we were dealing with something significantly stronger than what any of us suspected, and again, I reconsidered sending Chelsea into the attic.

No. We *needed* to do it. We were making paranormal history.

We needed it. She needed it.

Once I regained my breath, I held up a palm to the camera. "Wow. Let me just point out to you—quickly, if our cameraman, Don, will follow me here—that there are no open windows in the house, no fans, nothing that could have caused a draft to slam that door." I peeked in the master bedroom, then Chelsea's bedroom, then pointed to the window down at the end of the hallway, and had Don show the viewers that the bathroom window was also closed.

We were upstairs, and since it would take up too much valuable time, I had Mike reassure the audience that there were no open windows downstairs. "I closed them all myself," he said begrudgingly. At least he was playing along.

"That was pure, unadulterated paranormal energy, folks. All right, as I was saying—I'm just making sure that this door is propped open here—trigger objects are items we use to draw out spirits. If you'll remember from our episode in Tombstone, Arizona, we dressed up like outlaws and had a mock gunfight out in the street, shot blanks from our revolvers. That's a trigger *event* with trigger *objects*. Intelligent spirits can see us, they can interact, and it'll draw them out more if they're shown something familiar to them. That said, what we're about to do is unprecedented. Up here, directly above us in this very attic, resides one of the evilest, strongest demons we've ever encountered. We believe he—at least we *think* it's a he—has been torturing families who have attempted to live in this home for decades.

"Before the Hoppers, the Casons lived here. Before them, the Leyerzaphs, the Huttons, the Johnsons, all the way back to the 1850s when this home was built. Report after report after report, but none of them as terrifying as what the Hoppers had to endure. So what we're going to attempt is this: We're going to beat this thing with the white light of childhood innocence. We're going to send little Chelsea Hopper, who is only five years old, up into this attic. She's our trigger object. She's going to battle the demon that terrorized her for so long, and we're going to send it packing. We don't need a priest. We don't need holy water. We need unconditional love to battle the darkest rage."

I paused to take a breath. It was done. There would be no backing out.

As if he was reading my mind, Mike whispered, "Don't do this, Ford. I'm begging you."

I prayed that my mic didn't pick that up. We absolutely had to show solidarity. If we got cold feet, we'd be crucified throughout the Internet and the paranormal community. Our reputation, our credibility! Flush them like turds because we'd be a laughingstock if we lost our nerve during something so huge, right?

In my earpiece, another producer, Jack Hale, who was monitoring the feeds from the production truck, quietly said, "Holy fucking shit, Ford, we just passed eight million web viewers. Keep going. Knock this fucking thing out of the park."

Behind me, Mike said, "Ford?"

In front of me, Carla pinched her face into a point and shook her head, silently scolding him.

"Okay, let me remind you that this is live television," I said. "And here we go. Bring her up. Chelsea Hopper, ladies and gentlemen, our demon warrior."

Don panned the camera around to the stairwell, and the fans watching saw the same thing I did: a petite blonde child bouncing up the steps. It was hard to tell on screen, given the night-vision view, but she was wearing pink jeans with butterflies on the pockets, along with a white shirt bearing a rainbow-colored unicorn. Her shoes were the tiniest things, small enough to fit in a shirt pocket, and even in the pitch black of night, I could tell that she was smiling from ear to ear.

"Mr. Ford!" she said, darting down the hall toward me.

Damn it if my heart didn't turn into a mushy puddle, and I felt overpowering guilt, but the damage was already done. The boulder was picking up speed as it rolled down the hill. I squatted when she reached me and put my arm on her shoulder, turning her toward the camera. My hands were shaking.

Shy little Chelsea snickered and covered her mouth with her hands. She held them cupped together, almost like she was praying, and I wondered if she was old enough to understand the concept of God.

"Are you ready for this?" I asked. "Are you ready to go fight the—um, I mean, it's time to go beat up the bad guy, okay?"

I couldn't bring myself to say 'the dark man' because I knew she was afraid of him.

Chelsea seemed to retreat further into her hiding place behind her hands, then nodded in agreement.

"We're going to beat the bad guy together, okay? You remember what we talked about, and you'll be fine."

I stood up beside her.

Her head barely reached the middle of my thigh. She was so small.

That thing up in the attic was so strong.

I kept trying to convince myself that if she could face it down, the rest of her life would be a cakewalk. She'd be able to take on *anything*. I thought I believed it, but really, I just sounded desperate for my conscience to agree with me.

Mike slipped away like a ghost, out of the shot, leaving me to pull the cord. We'd been friends, partners, and brothers for years, and the look of disappointment on his face cut deeper than anything I could have imagined from him. It was sadness. Despair. Disbelief. I trusted Mike and his opinions. He had the right answers, always. Truth be told, I was the talent, he was the brains, and neither of us had a problem admitting it.

With my back to the camera, so that eight million people watching online and probably triple that watching on television at home couldn't see me, I mouthed the words "*I have to.*" Maybe it was an apology. A poor one.

He looked away.

I pulled the cord, and then I told Chelsea, "I'll be right here. You'll be fine."

When I glanced back at the camera, I had no idea that the image would be captured and used for weeks. That single picture of my face, a helpful grin distorted into some vile sneer, would portray *me* as the demon.

And, really, who would I be to argue?

# CHAPTER 10

When I get back to Mike and Craghorn, the front door is wide open, and they're cautiously looking back inside the house.

Well, Mike is, while Craghorn stands off to the side with his arms wrapped around his body. I have to get right on top of them before I realize that Mike is whispering the Lord's Prayer, like he's a member of a SWAT team tossing a smoke grenade inside before he storms the drug czar's hideout.

I wanted to tell him about the jogger and her shirt, but it doesn't seem like the right time. I'll save it for when I need an extra dose of good karma. Or there's a chance it'll work against me if I remind him of the good ol' days.

Anyway, Mike doesn't hear me come up the steps, and Craghorn doesn't acknowledge my presence. These facts combined send Mike three inches off the ground when I tap on his shoulder and say, "What's going on?"

Once he lands and the shock has drained from his face, he punches my shoulder. "Asshole."

"We even now?"

"Even? For what?"

"Remember that old church in France, beginning of season four? You caught me napping on one of the pews, thought it might be funny to teach me a lesson?"

He nods. "One of our highest-rated episodes. Partly because a few million people watched you piss your pants."

"Hey, I dribbled. It wasn't a full stream."

I'm aware that this banter isn't appropriate in front of Craghorn, so I cut the jawing and ask Mike if they uncovered any more details while I was gone.

Craghorn says nothing, as expected, and Mike tells me, "He says the right-hander didn't show up until after that maid—what was her name?"

"Elaine," I answer.

"The right-hander showed up after Elaine found the diary. Louisa had it buried underneath a floorboard up on the second floor. So what I'm thinking is, that diary was hidden down there where nobody could find it, and all that negative energy was trapped. Yeah? Make sense? So she's up there one day cleaning, finds a loose floorboard, and being the nosy type, she decides to investigate. Pulls the diary out and boom, it's like the Ark of the Covenant in Indiana Jones when the Germans open it up. All that black energy comes surging out, and Mr. Right-Hander, maybe he's hanging around the area, looking for a fresh snack, and there you go, moth to a flame."

I have to agree with him. He makes a perfectly good case for it, and that's probably a conclusion I could've come to on my own had either the detective or Craghorn told me the diary had been buried, or that the demon had just shown up around the time the maid found it.

Pardon the pun, but the devil is in the details.

First off, spirits can get attached to objects, like something that a person had an emotional connection with when they were on this side of the graveyard soil. More than likely, Louisa Craghorn was dumping every ounce of sentiment into this diary, keeping tabs on everything she was doing with Mayor Gardner, yet she also had a tremendous amount of guilt about what she was doing to her poor husband. All that negativity was swarming around her, enveloping her body and mind, soaking into those pages.

Second, if something like that has been secured away, all of that blackness can stay contained until, you guessed it, someone disturbs it. Once it's unleashed, it's free game, and it usually results in a haunting from a spirit who's been at rest for years, decades even. We in the paranormal community see it a lot, especially when someone moves into an old house and begins remodeling.

Tear down some drywall in your grandma's old house and see what happens.

That's common. What's rare is something else, something otherworldly, being close enough to detect that fresh batch of energy. It would be like hanging out on your front porch, and a neighbor three houses down is frying bacon, and you have no qualms about traipsing right into his kitchen to feast on it.

This whole scenario is apt to be the reason we captured Louisa Craghorn's voice, and the voice of the uninvited guest in their home. Louisa is here, and she wants to apologize, but more important, I'd bet she wants forgiveness. Even still, if Craghorn says, "You're forgiven," that thing in there won't let her leave. It's feeding off of her. It's feeding off of the negative energy it's creating in Craghorn, or completely sapping what's left of the positive kind.

91

All of this goes through my head in a flash, and I'm immediately caught up with Mike's train of thought.

I tell them, "Totally makes sense. So here's where we move forward. I just talked to Detective Thomas, and Mr. Craghorn, if it's okay with you, and if Mike is up for it, I think we'd like to perform a full investigation. I know we captured your wife's voice, and I know we heard that evil bastard in there, but I think we can squeeze more out of it. I think we can get you some real answers."

A flicker of excitement flashes across Mike's face. Then he tries, and fails, to hide it. That's all I needed to see. The dangling carrot did its job.

Fun fact: Mike actually hates carrots.

Craghorn lifts his eyes to meet mine, but nothing else comes with it, almost as if he's glowering at me from underneath his brow. His voice is quiet, though, when he asks, "What're you hoping to find?"

"More evidence. I let the detective know about what we caught in those EVPs—your wife's voice offering an apology, that right-hander saying she was guilty. Although it's not likely admissible, and what I do so rarely is, he feels like it still gives him enough to go on. Enough to continue pursuing the murder angle."

"Hang on," Mike says. "Just because she said 'I'm sorry' doesn't mean she was murdered. He's reaching."

"Yes and no. 'I'm sorry' could be an apology for anything. But he's going on the assumption that she's apologizing for the very reason we're here—the diary, the infidelity. And if it's a true thing, then it's enough of a clue for him to keep looking. So if you couple 'I'm sorry' with the right-hander calling her guilty, it's solid."

"Ford, you and I both know demons like that, especially the powerful ones. They'll use any form of trickery and deception they can to fuck with mortals."

"Exactly, which is why we need to investigate further." I turn to Craghorn and put my hand on his shoulder. He flinches as if the act delivers a small shock. I gently squeeze fragile bones. "My hope is that we can wrangle that demon into a corner long enough to ask your wife's spirit some questions. If we can make contact and get her to communicate clearly, she may be able to tell us who murdered her."

"I would like that," Craghorn says.

There's a tiny bell ringing way deep down in my psyche. Something is trying to get my attention, a gut sensation about this beaten-down man, and I can't place what it might be.

I leave my hand on Craghorn's shoulder a second too long. He looks down at it, then at me. He's so flat and expressionless.

And then it hits me—it feels like he's hiding information, and I make a mental note to ask Mike about this later.

It's strange, the way he's acting—so emotionless—but he's also had a top-tier demon sucking every ounce of vigor and life out of him for the past six months. Could be that the poor dude's tired.

"Mike?" I say. "You're in, right?"

He hesitates long enough to act like he's thinking it over, and then says yeah, but he'll have to call Toni and let her know he won't be home for supper. I can imagine how that conversation will go, considering the fact that *I'm* involved, and it won't be pretty. My guess is, he'll spend ten minutes trying to convince her that he's here to help Mr. Craghorn, and that I can go to hell after this is done, and it's only one investigation with me. She could use a girls' night out, right? He'll tell her all of this, but if I know Mike, and I do, he's quietly wiggling his excited bottom like Ulie staring down a treat.

Ulie. *Shit.* I'll need to call Melanie from wardrobe and check in on him. I told her I'd be back by midnight tonight. There's no way that's happening now. So it looks like I might need to do a little begging, too. She's not my biggest fan, if I haven't made that clear, but she tolerates my existence when I ask for help.

Her heart is bigger than her disgust.

When Mike leaves to call his wife, I'm left standing on the stoop with Craghorn. I don't want to pepper the guy with even more questions, especially after the detective and Mike have bombarded him, but until we get a chance to compare notes, it's a necessity.

But first I say, "We won't be bringing you in tonight, okay? This will strictly be just me and Mike."

Why? Because there's no way in hell I'm making the mistake of using someone who might be susceptible to a demonic entity as bait. Not again. I learned my lesson with Chelsea Hopper, and I'm still trying to atone for that.

I add, "You got somewhere to stay? Friends with an extra bedroom?"

"Friends," he replies, as if they're something he remembers from another life. "No. Not really. None that I've seen in years."

"Family in town?"

He shakes his head. "Dead or a thousand miles away."

"Okay, no big deal." I pull my wallet from my back pocket and fish out a couple of hundred dollar bills. "I'm staying at the Seaside down at the oceanfront. They know me there. Just ask for Delane at the front desk, tell her I sent you, and then book an oceanfront room. You mention me, she'll probably comp you a nice dinner in the restaurant. Go relax, Dave. Get away from this place for a while. You could use a recharge, yeah?"

There's no need to mention the fact that Delane is one of many reasons why Melanie from wardrobe is no longer Mrs. Ford Atticus Ford.

Craghorn's hand advances and retreats toward the bills, as if he's gingerly waiting on them to bite his fingertips, and then he takes them, folds them in half, and stuffs them in a pocket.

But not before I notice the scars. No wonder he's kept his hands in his pockets this whole time.

"Whoa, let me see."

"See what?"

"Your right hand."

"I . . . it's nothing."

He shows me anyway. It's mottled pink with raised flesh, scratch upon scratch.

I grit my teeth and wince. Some of them look fresh. Others have been there awhile. You would think that you couldn't get that many scars across the back of a single hand, but they're thin lines, crosshatched, like someone has been gouging him with a stickpin. I picture the razor-sharp point of a demonic claw, slowly dragging along, splitting flesh. One single, screeching nail on a chalkboard made of skin.

I grab the stretchy jacket fabric around his wrist and pull the sleeve up to his elbow. My heart sinks. This poor man. "Oh, buddy," I say, mimicking my mother when I got hurt as a child.

Craghorn's entire arm is covered in scratches, some new, some months old, and I don't have to ask about the rest of his frail body. I can see it in my mind already. I'm sure he's covered head to toe in claw marks. I doubt there's much skin left that isn't. He's not wearing a jacket and slacks in 104-degree heat because it's cold inside his house; he's wearing them because this goddamn thing has used him as a canvas.

"Get out of here," I say. "You leave, and don't you ever come back. We'll handle this."

# CHAPTER 11

Craghorn leaves, but not without protesting as much as he can muster, and I call Melanie from wardrobe to check on Ulie. She's not pleased that I've inconvenienced her yet again, but says she's okay with it, because of this: "Ulie is just the cutest wutest puppy wuppy in the whole wide world. Yes, he is! Who's the cutest puppy?"

The conversation stopped being directed at me about two minutes ago.

I say my goodbyes to the cutest puppy in the whole wide world and promise her that it'll only be one more night. She knows me, and she knows I can't keep that promise when I'm heavily involved in a case, and says as much.

"It's fine, Ford," she adds. "He's in puppy heaven. Doesn't even know you're gone."

Ouch. That stings, but I know that she's not really referencing Ulie. I'm sure his feelings are the conduit for what she's trying to tell me.

"Thanks, Mel," I say. "I'll get back as soon as I can."

"Any word on Chelsea's story?"

She knows that any moment I'm not working for The Man—like, literally, the cops, government agents—I spend my time trying to find, and destroy, the thing that hurt that little girl. "I went back out to that farmhouse right before I came to Virginia."

"Any luck?"

"Helluva lot better than last time. Listen, Mike's coming. I'll tell you about it when I come to pick up Ulie. It's good. Big time. Could help a lot if I ever get a damn chance to follow up on it."

"Wait, hang on. Did you say Mike? As in, Mike *Long*?"

"Yeah."

"One sec, let me check the news."

"For what?"

"I didn't hear anything about the world ending."

"Funny. Oh, hardy har, hardy har."

"He's actually there. With you. On a job," she says, not like it's a question, but as a statement of absolute disbelief regarding a true fact.

"He lives down in Kitty Hawk, remember? And *this*, Jesus, Mel, this is *big*. Whatever's in this house, it's as bad as that right-hander that got Chelsea. Maybe even stronger." I almost tell her about the marks all over Craghorn's body, but I change my mind. I don't want her to worry about me. You know, since I'm foolishly thinking she'll care. "I *need* Mike's help. Seriously. So I called, and amazingly enough, he came."

I can hear her sigh. "For only the second time, the almighty Ford Atticus Ford has met something he can't tame." I can't tell if she's talking about the demon, or herself. That's a long story for another chapter. I'm still hunting the ghosts of our marriage. Maybe they can tell me what went wrong. Maybe they can give me answers.

Not about what happened, really, because I know what I did.

About why I let someone like her go.

I'd like to ask them what I was thinking, because I have no clue.

"Yeah," I say. It's the only thing that makes sense.

"Tell Mike I said hi and to behave himself."

"Apparently he's off the sauce. I don't think we'll have to worry about that too much."

"I meant for him not to kill you tonight. He wouldn't last long in prison."

"Jokes galore today, huh?"

"It's a necessary evil around you, my friend. Okay, Ford. Call me when you get into town. Ulie misses you."

And for about half a second, for the teeniest, tiniest moment, I hope that this statement might not be about the dog, either.

I hang up. It's not and never will be. I done screwed up good.

Thunder grumbles in the distance. It would be nice if a rain shower came through and cooled things down a bit, but most likely what'll happen is, it'll rain for five minutes, just enough to soak this concrete jungle. And here, this close to the ocean with the humidity sitting at about 7,000 percent, it'll do nothing more than turn all of Hampton Roads into a suffocating sauna.

I'm almost looking forward to the freezing air inside the Craghorn compound.

But not really, considering the thing causing it might finally commit me to an insane asylum.

I turn my eyes away from the dark clouds shouldering out the blue sky on the horizon and see Mike walking toward me. His expression is glum. He looks like he went a few rounds with Tyson and finally managed to crawl off the mat long after the match ended.

"Didn't go over so well, huh?" I ask.

"Well, I got permission, but if you ask me, there was another right-hander on the other end of that line. She was *not* happy."

"Not my biggest fan anymore?"

He chuckles and shakes his head. "As if she ever was."

"Good point."

"She'll never forgive you for Chelsea."

"Her and about forty million people." I let that simmer a moment. Then I ask him, "Have you?"

"Forgiven you?"

"Yeah."

"What do you think?"

His tone suggests I already know the answer. I do, but it was worth a shot, regardless.

I have to wipe the layer of sweat from my forehead. It's now mixed with hair gel that seems to be melting off my damn head and leaves my hand gooey. I fling away the droplets, and the remainder gets swiped down my pants leg. Pretty sure that my trademark black from head-to-toe outfit was the worst idea imaginable in this heat. Right about now, I'm praying that storm in the distance makes its way here. I'd love to have about five minutes of relief before we go tackle this beast.

I ask Mike if Craghorn showed him any of his scars earlier.

"Not until I asked. He wanted to show me how the doorbell would ring by itself at all hours of the night.

Caught me looking at the scars on his hands, and I made him show me what else had been done to him. I wanted to ask you about it because something felt weird."

I pantomime pulling a sleeve back. "He showed you, right? Whole arm was covered, both sides."

"Not just his arms. Nearly everything."

"Yeah? I thought his entire body would be covered."

"What're we gonna do about him?"

"He's already gone." I point my chin east, in the direction of the ocean, and tell Mike that I sent Craghorn away. "Gave him money for a night's stay at the Seaside—"

"Delane still there?"

"Yeah, but that's not—forget it. Doesn't matter."

"So what's he doing after we're finished? What happens if we can't get rid of this right-hander on our own? It'll take a while to convince the Catholics to come down for an exorcism, and, even then, there's no guarantee. He *can't* come back here. Does he have family? Friends?"

"We already went over all that, and no, he doesn't. I'll figure something out."

I've been known to help out a client on occasion if I'm moved enough by their story, but rarely do I commit myself this deeply. Mike and I made a lot of money in sponsorships and advertisements for The Paranormal Channel, and, in turn, we were extremely well compensated for it. Truthfully, I wouldn't ever have to work again if I chose not to, but I have questions that remain and a little girl to avenge.

What I'm trying to say is, I have plenty of offshore accounts and investments that I can tap into. If Dave

Craghorn needs a new place to live, I can afford to set him up until he gets rid of the deep shadows that are sucking away the light in his life. Nobody deserves that.

Mike says, "You know, I don't get you, Ford. I'm not sure I ever did or ever will."

"How so?"

"I get what you're saying. I know exactly what you're talking about. You'll buy that guy a freakin' house on the oceanfront if it means taking care of him. You got a good heart, but damn if it ain't tainted black once in a while."

"You mean Melanie? Cheating?"

"That's part of it, yeah. How many were there? Ten? Fifteen?"

"Six," I admit, angling the word out in a tone that suggests, 'Hey, it wasn't *that* bad.'

"One is all it takes. Anyway," he says, checking the sky as thunder barrels through, "it's more than just screwing up with Melanie. The greed, the motivation, stepping all over people on our way to the top, sending Chelsea into—never mind. This ain't about her. It's about—"

"It's *always* been about her. At least since TPC yanked the show."

"Let me finish," Mike says. A sprinkle of rain splats against my cheek. "What I'm trying to say is, it will never make any goddamn sense to me how you can buy some poor soul a house with your own money, or cut a check for a couple mil' to some kid's charity, and then you turn right around and grind something into hamburger if you think it'll get you somewhere. I don't *get* it. I don't know how you live with yourself, and I don't know what motivates you to pay attention to the angel on your shoulder one day, and the devil the next."

Mike is right. He's always right. But I'm not ready to admit it.

Plus, I don't know what the answer is either—faulty wiring, perhaps.

It's funny how this is the most he's ever opened up to me, especially on the back of a two-year separation. It sounds as if he's been practicing this for a while, and no matter how much he says he's only here to help Craghorn, I feel like he was looking for an opportunity to get this little speech off his chest. Maybe Toni got tired of listening to him recite it in front of a mirror.

*No, Ford, be nice. Could be a distant attempt at forgiveness.*

But, given a second to think about it, maybe I shouldn't get that confused with pity.

Whatever. I'm glad to have him back.

I spend too much time analyzing things these days.

Best to let this discussion go to voice mail.

I slap Mike on the back, heartily, like old pals, and say, "Okay then. Nice chat. Now let's go hunt some fucking ghosts."

*** 

Mike and I go through our standard routine, and it's fluid, like we never hopped off the bicycle. He's wax on; I'm wax off. Easy as it ever was. He runs a baseline EMF check to see if there are any unnatural electromagnetic spikes that might cause a sensation of being watched and things of that nature. You get too much EMF humming around your body and brain, there's a good possibility that it can cause visual distortions, even hallucinations. Some people are more sensitive than others, and that's the way it is. No rhyme or reason.

We had a janitor in Minnesota one time who was working around enough EMF juice to fry an egg. He never noticed. But then, there was a woman in Northern California who had a minimal spike in her laundry room whenever she turned on the washing machine. She would faint from the EMF buzzing around her and claim that whole hordes of angry spirits were trying to have an orgy with her. Fun stuff.

But, on the other hand, a hungry spirit can also soak up this EMF energy and use it to communicate. We even have what we call an "EMF Pump" that we'll deploy sometimes in an attempt to supercharge the atmosphere. Neither Mike nor I have one with us at the moment, but given the strength of this razor-clawed entity that's already here, I doubt we'll need it.

It won't be fully dark for at least another three hours, so it's beneficial to us to get all of the standard objectives out of the way while we can still see.

By the time Mike finishes the routine EMF scope downstairs and comes up empty, I already have three of his "spotcams" situated in assorted positions. Various paranormal groups have their pet terms for what they call these stationary filming units, but they're really just digital cameras on tripods that are set to record in night vision from a static location. One spot all night, thus, the *spot*cam.

We even had a group of die-hard *Graveyard: Classified* fans who dubbed themselves the "spotcamgirls." The pictures they sent to our e-mail address at The Paranormal Channel headquarters would make a porn star blush, much less the unfortunate intern who answered all of our mail for minimum wage.

Maybe he didn't mind so much.

Glory days, indeed.

"Looks like you've got them in good locations," Mike says.

"Yeah, the one there in the eastern corner picks up the entire living room where Craghorn was attacked earlier today, plus that entrance down into the kitchen where he was watching something while I talked to the detective." I move over to the next one and wave down the hallway. "This one will capture anything along this whole corridor—living room, kitchen, storage closet off in the peripheral with a direct line of sight down to the back door. It's all covered. Then the third one over here is set up in the top corner of the stairwell, looking up at where Craghorn told you he hears footsteps all night long, and then right over to the entrance. It's all set up like a funnel down here, herding everything in front of a camera."

Damn, that felt good. There for a minute, I was totally in the zone with Don the cameraman behind me and Charlie Chocolate Chip, the sound guy, standing off to the side and holding a small boom mic over my head, while I explained to the fans and casual viewers how we were setting up to conduct the investigation. Back a couple of years ago, I would've nailed the whole thing on the first take.

"Ford?" Mike says, bringing me out of the revelry in my mind.

"Huh?"

"You got a little gleam in your eye. Right there in the corner."

"Sorry. Reminiscing."

"Doesn't change anything, but I felt it, too. Did you ever think about—*Jesus Christ*!"

We duck, throwing our heads down and to the side as a decorative ceramic plate hurtles past our heads.

Bewildered, mouth agape, Mike straightens up and asks, "Where in the hell did that come from?"

I look behind us. The plate lies on the hardwood floor, smashed to pieces against the grandfather clock that's been dead for decades, according to Craghorn. "That looks like the Elvis plate," I tell him. "One of those commemorative ones. It used to be in the kitchen, hanging beside the refrigerator. I noticed it because my mom used to have the same one."

In the silence between our breathing, my ear picks up an intruding sound.

It's a distant noise, the staccato rhythm of slow-stepping hooves.

Clop, clop. Clop, clop.

I picture the demon walking down the hall behind me. I strain to listen for the hooves. The hair on my arms stands at attention. The pressing pain in my bladder builds.

Then I realize the sound isn't coming from far away. It's right beside me. It's the dead clock ticking.

Now *that* is an omen.

# CHAPTER 12

We're standing up on the second floor, at the head of the stairs, looking back down toward the front entryway where the decorative plate lies in ruins. We left it alone as a small symbol of defiance, just enough to flip the bird at the right-hander to let him, or her, or it, know that we weren't going to bend to its will.

*You* break something and *we* clean it up?

As if.

Well, I mean, not until the investigation is over. We won't really leave a mess for Craghorn *if* he ever comes home. God, I hope he won't. I hope he listens to what I said and stays far, far away from this place.

Mike holds a thermal imaging camera, and what this thing does is, it takes all of the ambient heat in the room and projects it as an image on a small screen. All the warm stuff is displayed in reds, pinks, oranges, and yellows. Imagine the stages of a sunset; that's what the room temperature heat looks like, more or less. Now, a spiritual presence is typically cold because it's sucking energy out of the atmosphere in order to manifest, so if you're looking at the screen and you see a dark mass, or figure, whatever, as it's walking across the room, there's a damn good chance you've got company.

I wait with my arms crossed, patiently and silently. "Anything?"

Mike breathes heavily through his nose. He's always done that. That's a sound I haven't heard in a long time. It's like going home again.

He answers, "Nothing. But it's already so cold in here that it would almost be hard to tell the difference."

"Would it help to switch it over to black and white?"

Same concept, only instead of a rainbow differentiating heat discrepancies, you have a monochromatic representation. It has its uses, but I prefer all the pretty colors.

He flips a switch, turns a couple of dials and, yeah, lots of black. That doesn't do much for us.

"Should we move on?"

"Five more minutes. I want to see if that thing is stalking us."

In all honesty, we sort of *retreated* up to the second floor. That's not something I'm fond of admitting but when you have a right-hander powerful enough to sling breakable things at your head, it might be a good idea to get out of the way.

Technically, we could classify it as poltergeist activity. However, it's not like there are a bunch of cabinet doors flying open and dead-battery toys dancing around the room. This demon is strong enough, and focused enough, and intuitive enough, to lift one single object—an object that caught my attention earlier in the day—and sling it over thirty-five feet.

That's not just an explosion of paranormal energy.

That's *intent*.

Mike inhales and exhales; the tempo of his body rocks like a persistent metronome. I want to be hunting for this thing, calling it out, telling it to come fight us, but it's good to ease into an investigation like this. We have all night, and it feels like we're getting back into our groove. Mike was always the one who focused more on the technical side of the investigation. Devices, gadgets, cameras, you name it, we tried it.

Back in the day, and it looks to be shaping up the same way, he was James Bond and I was Oprah.

You know, gadgets versus emotion. He's pushing buttons, tweaking dials, and I'm riling up the crowd: You get a demonic possession! You get a demonic possession! *You* get a demonic possession! *Everybody* gets a demonic possession!

"Ford?"

"What?"

"Did you hear that?"

"No? Maybe?"

Mike hasn't peeled his eyes away from the thermal imager screen yet, but he's clearly focused on something as he lifts an arm and points over his back, which is also to my rear. I hate to be sneaked up on. Frazzles me, waiting on something to pounce.

One thing I never understood was how our cameramen, Don in particular, could stand there with a camera focused on Mike and me while we were freaking out about something happening behind them. They were brave, man. Never flinching, never wavering—it was always about the shot, capturing our reactions. I argued with the producers for over a decade that our fans wanted to see what we were looking at. They didn't want to see *us* having an absolute shit-fit when a shadow figure darted across an empty gymnasium. The spirits were the real show, not us, but the producers, Carla in particular, didn't see it that way.

I spin around and take a couple of steps to put my back closer to the wall. "What was it?"

"Sounded like a voice. Couldn't tell from where. Female, probably, and I'd bet your beach house in the Hamptons that it's Louisa again." He finally looks over at me and drops the thermal imaging camera to his side. "I got nothing downstairs. Whatever it was ain't there anymore. Should we go check out the voice?"

"Yeah. And the Hamptons house is gone, by the way. Melanie from wardrobe got it in the divorce; turned right around and sold the damn thing for about nine million."

Mike puts his hands on his hips, shakes his head like a disappointed father.

"What?"

He hooks a thumb down toward the far bedroom and starts walking. "Did you ever think that maybe one of the *other* reasons she left you, aside from cheating on her six fucking times, was because you couldn't take the relationship seriously?"

Defiant, I say, "What's that supposed to mean? Of course I took it seriously. Kinda."

"Dude, you never stopped calling your *wife* 'Melanie from wardrobe.'"

"Not to her face." But, again, he has a point. "That was habit, nothing more. That's who she was for six years before we started dating."

"And then, things changed. You didn't respect her."

"This is *not* a discussion I feel like having, okay? We're here to help Craghorn, not dissect my failed marriage. I'm not on Oprah."

"What?"

"Forget it."

As we stand in front of the bedroom door, Mike gives me a sharp look and says, "She's a good girl, Ford. You ruined it. Just like you managed to ruin everything else."

It stings to hear it, out loud, *again*, but I'm not going to argue with him. One, I don't feel like it and two, I have no counterpoint. I open my mouth, and I'm about to tell him to leave my personal life out of the hunt when we both hear it.

A soft moaning comes from the second guest bedroom at our backs. We turn, ready and guarded, cocking our heads, listening intently, glancing at each other sideways. It's definitely female, and it does indeed have the same tone and pitch as what Mike caught on his digital recorder earlier. He lifts a finger to his lips, gently taps out a shush, hands me the thermal imager, and then reaches into his back pocket to pull out his GS-5000, which is the big brother to the BR-4000 I accidentally left at home. This thing is the Cadillac of digital voice recorders. Real time audio playback so you can ask questions while you record and hear any responses. If you do happen to catch something, you can skip back and listen to it while the secondary mic continues ahead. It's a brilliant device.

He lifts it, presses the button with the red circle on it, and pantomimes instructions. He's going to push open the door while I use the thermal imager to immediately capture what's in the room. I feel a bit like we're a couple of real badge-carrying detectives ourselves, and we're about to bust in on a most-wanted criminal snorting coke out of a hooker's butt crack.

I spend a lot of time in hotels. Maybe I watch too much television.

Mike lifts his hand, reaches for the door, and pauses. Frozen in place, he says, "Whoa, hang on," and then— "*Hungh!*"

He flies into me, sideways, and we both stumble to our left and land hard. My back crashes into a weakly constructed, triple-drawer console table, and the thing explodes under my weight, sending two picture frames and a decorative jewelry box onto my head and chest.

Mike lands off-kilter, holding his GS-5000 up high to keep from smashing it, and cracks his head against the hardwood floor.

I fling bits of splintered table and an empty drawer off me and climb to my knees, clambering over to Mike. "Holy shit. What happened? You okay?" I'm whipping my head around, trying, and failing, to see if another ambush is coming.

Instead of answering, Mike pushes himself up and crab walks back to the wall. We both know who did it—the question is where did it go? Are we still in danger?

I ask him again if he's okay, if he's hurt, either from falling or from the attack, and once he's satisfied that he's not going to get another beating, he tells me everything's fine, to back off a second.

"Okay, but just—"

"I'm good, Ford," he insists. "God, that was intense. I just need a minute. *Please.*"

I sit on my haunches and watch him, checking for anything out of the ordinary. Unusual anger, confusion, a feeling of immediate dread. You know, head-spinning, pea-soup-spitting type stuff. With a *blitzkrieg* that powerful, I'm worried that the right-hander attacked, invaded, and then put up a set of nice linen curtains in its new home, 123 Mike Long Street.

He understands what I'm doing, too, because he holds a palm up to me and says, "Just chill, man. I don't feel anything."

"Promise?"

"Yeah. It's not like that time in Miami."

Some people might go to Miami and come home with a sunburn or an STD. Mike went down for a solo investigation while I was on my honeymoon with Melanie from wardrobe—sorry, *Melanie*—and came home with a stowaway. He got careless, didn't protect himself going in or coming out, warning the entities that he was *not* a vessel, and it took days of prayer with one of the big guns from the Vatican and three Native American shamans to get his body, mind, and home clear again. Toni wasn't too happy about that, and, somehow, per standard operating procedure, she managed to find a way to blame me.

115

Melanie and I were on a rinky-dink motorbike in the jungles of Vietnam when it happened, but, yeah, it was my fault. Thanks, Toni.

I remind him how much that experience sucked and make him promise to tell me if he feels anything out of the ordinary over the next few hours. I add, "You know the drill, Mike. Depression, murderous ideas."

He rubs the back of his head where it hit the floor and checks for blood on his fingertips. Hand clean, he says, "You mean murderous ideas directed toward you?"

"Yeah."

"That's not out of the ordinary, Ford. That's a Tuesday."

I laugh. Mike laughs.

And for a moment, it's good. That would've been a prime capture for the show. A speck of levity to break the ungodly tension right before a commercial break.

*Your sheets will be as white as ghosts with new clothesline-scented Sparkle Clean.*

While I'm picturing that kid in the red T-shirt and gray jeans as he runs around with the blanket on his head—acting like a ghost, as expected—Mike hums a few bars of the commercial's theme song.

Yeah. We're back. I'd like to high-five him, but it's slightly creepy how connected we are.

Are? Were? I'm not sure where we stand.

He pushes himself to his feet, and I get up with him.

"Should we check?" I ask. He's already lifting his shirt before I finish the sentence. I wince and hiss. "That's a good one."

"Burns like hell."

"Ha ha."

"No, man, I'm serious. My skin is on fire. Look at the welts."

There's a big splotch on the right side of his rib cage. It's bright pink and getting redder, along with five raised welts and a mottled mound that looks like a palm. It's a handprint, for sure, but it's not human.

"You smell that?" Mike asks sniffing the air.

"Yeah. Your skin smells like brimstone."

# CHAPTER 13

The thing about being a standard, run-of-the-mill private investigator is that they can gather *tangible* evidence, which, mostly, comes in the form of pictures, videos, testimony, and other concrete things wherein a judge will look at it, nod his bald little head, waggle his floppy, loose-skinned jowls and say, "You have proved that Bill is sleeping with Tina, and Jane is entitled to forty bajillion dollars."

Or, rather, the house in the Hamptons and other valuables.

The point is, they can collect material proof that can be used in a court of law.

Me? What I do as a *paranormal* private investigator? It requires more finesse and deductive reasoning, not to mention the fact that the field of paranormal research remains *persona non grata* in most scientific circles. I don't care how many full-bodied apparitions I've seen, how many voices I've heard from beyond the grave, or how many pictures I've taken where a translucent man is standing off to the right of somebody's kitchen table, the general public, minus our legions of believers and fans, will look down their noses at it and say, "Yeah, but you could've faked that. See right here? The bottom of the door is off camera.

Who's to say you didn't tie a piece of fishing line to it and yank it closed from across the room?"

That's what Mike and I, and the rest of our crew, had to battle every single day while the show was running, and it's what I deal with now during each investigation, and it's why my work would hold as much water as a sieve if it were taken to the US legal system.

I often spend days on location, poring over historical records, interviewing potential witnesses and clients, conducting investigations, filming dark bedrooms and hallways, taking pictures, and being sneaky. The difference is, the people I'm trying to talk to are dead.

And the dead don't always cooperate—at least not fully. It's rare that I can walk into a home where someone has been murdered, fire up the old cameras and recorder, and hear a spirit on the other end of the line say, "It was Ronald James from accounting; he's the one who slit my throat." As a matter of fact, I think that's only happened once in the two years I've been contracting as a paranormal private investigator.

And it wasn't Ronald James from accounting, actually. It was Ted, down in the mailroom, because we all know the mailroom is where the creepy people work.

Okay, so, the point I'm trying to make is, sometimes during an investigation, I can say, "My name is Ford Atticus Ford, and I'm here to talk to Amanda Wallace. Amanda, if you're here, can you tell me where your husband hid your body?" and I'll get a vague response like, "He left me . . . She told him to."

Right there is an extra clue that the police can use. After friends and family members have authenticated that it's Amanda's voice, then begins the process of tracking down this "she" that Amanda mentioned. The family, the lawyers, the police, none of them had any clue that there was (potentially) a mistress or a girlfriend on the side, and if not that, a puppet master pulling the strings to help collect an insurance settlement, etc.

The courts won't accept it, but the detectives can choose to believe or ignore what I give them. Occasionally, they dismiss my evidence because even though they called me in to assist them in their investigation, they refuse to believe they could have missed something so simple. And then, when I'm out of sight, they'll follow it anyway. They're not stupid, just prideful.

If they do accept the validity of my data, it opens up an entirely new line of questioning and potential leads.

Because, like I've always said, dead people see things that others don't.

Sometimes it's that easy. Sometimes a spirit will muster enough energy and come through to our side and avenge his own death. Other times, I establish communication, but it's gibberish. Perhaps a family member can watch a video I've captured where a plant moves two inches, and then the sound of footsteps follow. It doesn't prove that Harold Bigelow choked Mrs. Harold Bigelow to death in a fit of murderous rage. What it proves, according to the family member, is that Mrs. Bigelow has come back from the grave, and she's still trying to position that plant exactly how she wanted it, against Harold's demands. It's proof that she's around, but it's not proof of her husband's guilt nor is it proof of his innocence.

Looking back on my case history, it's about a forty-sixty split between usable evidence and tangential proof of the afterlife.

I mention this because after we're finished examining the seared handprint on Mike's side, he lets me listen to the recording. He'd said, "Whoa, hang on," about a half second before the demonic linebacker caused a fumble on the one-yard line, and now, as we stand here in the hallway and listen to the rest of the recording, I get chills when the EVP comes through.

*"Ford . . . death . . ."*

It's a growl more than words, and I imagine that the voice is coated in thousands of years of soot and has been charred by the fires of hell.

Dramatic? Maybe. Sometimes I still picture myself talking to our viewership in my mind.

I cringe and lift an eyebrow at Mike. He returns it.

I take it to mean this right-hander is threatening my life, and it's freaking spooky, yet if I had given up and tucked-tail out the front door every time this happened, I would've quit, oh, about a thousand investigations ago.

We listen to it twice more and note that it comes in over top of the soft, female voice we'd heard that drew us to the room in the first place. That tells us a couple of things: one, this demonic entity didn't lure us into a trap, because sometimes they impersonate things they aren't, like children or a distressed family member, and two, that being noted, there is definitely more than one spiritual presence in this house.

We had already established this, more or less, but this is legitimate proof for Mike and me. It changes the direction of the impending overnight investigation now that we know for sure what we're dealing with.

Mike stops the playback and checks his watch. "What're we thinking? Another hour, hour and a half before total sundown? If that?"

"Probably so. I'd say we run a couple more baseline checks up here on this floor and the attic, just to be safe. Can't hurt to clear up all the variables."

"Yeah, and maybe if we find an EMF hotspot, we can target that location a little more than the dead zones. Craghorn told me that he often sees a lot of action in his bedroom and—oh for God's sake, Ford. Are you thirteen years old?"

"Sorry, it was just the way you phrased it. *Action* in the bedroom? Huh? Huh? C'mon."

"And Carla would have put that in an episode, and we would have spent the next week under a mountain of dick and fart jokes online." He scoffs, but he can't quite hide his grin. "I'm going to do the baseline EMF. Why don't you do a little recon around here and see if you can find anything he didn't tell us about?"

"On it." He doesn't have to tell me what he's thinking about, because we're operating like the machine of old, back in the saddle, and whatever cliché you can come up with. "Be careful," I add, hesitant to leave him completely alone after such a violent attack. But he's been working out, so he should be good.

Mike heads west, back in the direction of the spare bedrooms, and I go east to the front of the house. The giant bay window lets in the waning evening light, and the semitranslucent curtains hanging on an ancient iron rod do little to provide cover. They remind me of the ones back at the Hampstead farmhouse, which makes me all the more eager to get home and follow up on the leads I uncovered with Ulie the night before I came here.

A floorboard screeches under my feet, the wail of a dying animal, and I step away from it. In case Mike is running the recorder, I verbally mark the location and that it originated from me.

The odor up here is different than downstairs. Nothing bad, really, but nothing good either, like Craghorn hasn't aired it out in a couple of years. It's stale, musty, and I'm tempted to open the tall, double rectangular windows beside the big bay window, the kind that open with an L-shaped crank, and then I spot the taillights of traffic outside.

Nah, better not. The street noise could easily contaminate our investigation, so I suffer with the smell of dust and air with an expiration date from the Nixon administration.

I'm taking my time here, soaking it all up, trying to get inside Craghorn's head, hoping to give some substance to his reasons for staying here ten years after his wife was possibly murdered, and then six long months after a goddamn powerful right-hander moved in like that houseguest who never gets the hint that he needs to leave.

For as long as I have been doing this, I'll never understand why people allow themselves to be tortured. Sure, there are extenuating circumstances, like money issues, no family around, no place to go, along with a million other possibilities, but for the love of God, there *has* to be something you can do. If it were me, I would do whatever it took to get my wife, my husband, the kids, and the cat as far away from pure evil as I possibly could.

It took the Hoppers longer than it should have, but they were smart.

Eventually.

They left. They got Chelsea out.

And then this son of a bitch right here came along and brought her back.

*Argh, Ford, stop it. There's nothing you can do about it this very second. You're working on fixing things. It's a process.*

I have to mentally acknowledge this on a daily basis, roughly 2.3 million times. My therapist tells me it's a good thing to remind myself that we all make mistakes.

A *mistake* is putting pepper in the saltshaker.

What I allowed to happen was *unforgiveable*.

The upstairs hall seems fairly normal on this end. No new revelations into the mind of Craghorn. I hear Mike fumbling around in the office and listen for a moment. He sounds like he's fine, but damn, I'm worried. You take a hit like that from an upper level right-hander, it'll shake you for a while, especially if you've been off the bicycle for a spell like Mike has. If I send him home with a demon in his backpack, Toni might track me down and murder me.

If that happened, I'd come back and haunt her personally, because how perfect would that be?

Satisfied that my former partner, best friend, and brother-from-another-mother is okay back there by himself, I reach for the door handle closest to me. It's warm, like ten or twenty degrees warmer than the rest of this freezing house. The temperature isn't hot enough to burn me, however, but that doesn't stop me from jerking my hand away like I'm grabbing a rattlesnake by the tail. The foreign sensation—heat, I mean—is a surprise.

Normally, I'd check it out with the thermal imaging camera, but the damn thing is all the way over there on the banister, and besides, I already know it's a different temperature. I'm a bit concerned that something might be on fire in there, so rather than opening the door and fueling it with a fat, fresh supply of oxygen, I drop down to all fours and try to peek underneath the crack. I haven't done this since seventh grade when Teddy Martin's sister was changing out of her bikini.

I didn't see anything then, of course, unlike now, when a set of shadowy legs scamper across the room.

I recoil and jump back to my feet, unsure of what I saw. My hands go numb with excitement.

This is it.

This is the kind of stuff I live for, regardless of the investigations I'm on or what I'm trying to accomplish for some police department detective that I'll never see again.

There's something in there, something otherworldly, and I can barely contain myself as I call out to Mike and tell him to hurry.

# CHAPTER 14

Mike touches the doorknob and feels the difference in temperature. Like me, he yanks his arm back. "Yowsa." He checks the palm of his hand, perhaps instinctively, and asks me what room it is.

"Is this the one where Craghorn said his wife painted? Maybe? And I didn't even get a chance to check out the library and the sitting room over there on the right." I look past Mike at the two rooms, whose doors are open, and don't see anything scuttling around in there. "Should we check them out before we go in here for battle?"

"Are you nuts? Why're you not in there already? The old Ford would've run in there with a Ouija board and a handful of batteries like he was handing out Halloween candy."

"That giant clawed handprint on your side makes this one a little different."

Because, honestly, while this is what I live for, I also have no intention of dying for it, either.

He nods. "Good point, but we gotta do it."

"Rock-paper-scissors?"

Mike calls me a pansy, but not in the G-rated way, twists the doorknob, and pushes it open slowly. The moaning hinges are horror-movie creepy, and I wouldn't be surprised if a rattling skeleton dropped from the ceiling. Gotcha!

Instead, ropes of heated air crawl through the space, bringing with them the scent of something ancient. I have no way to describe the putrid aroma. It's as if something slithered out of a crypt that had been buried a thousand years ago. I recognize it as the faint, musty smell I noticed earlier, only now it's overwhelmingly pungent and sends my hand up over my nose and mouth.

Otherwise, the inside of the room is perfectly normal. It's another bedroom. There's a single bed with the long side against the wall. A flowery comforter lies on top of it, pristinely pressed, and a pillow with an equally wrinkle-free pillowcase sits at the head. There's a bare bookcase that I would expect to be covered in dust. It's not. It's spotless. A clear vase, filled halfway with water, holds daffodils in front of a square-paned window.

A tic-tac-toe window.

Sometimes I'm a poet and I know it.

There's a small desk underneath, which looks to be something straight off an Ikea showroom floor. It's white, square, and plainly made. A matching chair accompanies it. The surface is also free of everything, including dust, and to our left is a 1970s-style love seat that could be nothing other than the matching unit to the couch downstairs.

Mike grunts and lifts the collar of his shirt over his nose. "Shields up."

I don't see any sign of the previous occupant—the Thing of the Scuttling Legs—and I have to admit, going against my earlier sentiments, I'm slightly disappointed. It's always such a rush when you walk into a room and either catch an entity off guard, or spook something that's hiding, and then watch as it freaks out while it tries to get away from you.

We both notice the one odd thing in the room, simultaneously, and move over to the loose floorboard beside a hole. Mike, who is never without the proper equipment, produces a miniature flashlight from his Batman-style tool belt, flicks it on, and shines it down into the orifice. It's only about three inches wide, which means that craning my neck to see around Mike is doing no good. I wait until he's finished examining it and then ask for the light.

I don't know what I was expecting. Maybe a pentagram drawn in blood or the remnants of an animal sacrifice, something, anything evil.

It's empty. Completely and entirely empty. It's nothing but a hole that's bordered by dusty joists with the splintery subflooring as its bottom.

Then it occurs to me. "Oh, shit. This is probably where the maid found the diary."

"Yeah, that's what I was thinking."

"She popped this open and unleashed all that negative energy. You think that's why it smells so disgusting in here?"

"Nah, I'd say that's the right-hander. This is where he hangs out." Mike looks around the room at nothing in particular. "You hear me, you son of a bitch? You smell like shit! A big, stinking pile of ass goo, and once we're done, we're going to send you right back to the bottom of Satan's toilet where you belong."

"Yeah, Mike. Get 'im." I can't help myself. It's the Mike that I remember. The Mike that drove the ratings through the roof for any episode where he lost his cool and got all primeval on a spirit that pushed him too far. Carla and her marketing team were brilliant when it came to teasing those episodes with dark, gritty commercials. "*On this week's very special episode of* Graveyard: Classified, *the spirit world will finally experiences the wrath of Mike Long.*"

Truth be told, the spirit world "finally experienced" the wrath of Mike Long roughly twelve times over the course of the show's run. I'm pretty sure there was only one guy who e-mailed to tell us we sounded like a broken record. I sent him an autographed headshot and never heard from him again.

"You feel that?" Mike asks.

"What?"

"The temperature. Feels like it's back to normal." He checks the black box in his hand. "EMF is back to normal. Zero-point-zero. And what's that smell? It's like clean laundry."

"We scared it out of here. Damn thing retreated."

Mike shouts, "Coward!" at the ceiling.

"What now?"

"The usual. Wait until nightfall. Then we get ready for battle."

\*\*\*

I can tell that, in most respects, Mike is far from being my bestest buddy in the whole wide world again, but I do manage to talk him into joining me for dinner. After everything that's happened today, I need a break, and I'm in desperate need of some fuel before we gear up for war.

Mike balked for a bit, telling me he was only here on business, and all he wanted to do was help Craghorn get his life back. Reluctantly, he agreed to come along when I said he could pick the restaurant.

And so, here we sit at McCracken's Crab Hut.

Mike knows I'm deathly allergic to seafood.

Very funny.

While he mows down the largest bucket of crab legs I've ever seen, I convince our amazingly attractive waitress, who goes by the awkward name Caribou, to run over to the deli across the street and get me a Black Forest ham and swiss on rye. There's no denying that she recognizes the both of us, which seems to be exactly why she was willing to help me out. Or it could be the fact that if I so much as touch a plate that's had seafood on it, I'll blow up like a crimson pufferfish and go into convulsions, and that's not a good visual for the other patrons.

I'm even sitting here about a foot back from the table, trying to avoid any potential crab juice flying my way as Mike plows through the crab legs like a wood chipper shredding an oak branch.

The kind, generous, sweet, and in-no-way-trying-to-kill-me Caribou arrives with a hoagie-shaped object wrapped in white deli paper. It doesn't appear to be on rye bread, but she's forgiven when I notice that underneath the clear tape holding the wrapping closed is a perfectly smooched set of lips.

Sealed with a kiss. Nice.

She winks at me, says to enjoy my meal—on the house—and when she walks away, I can't help but notice the pert and perfectly shaped—

"Ford."

"Hmm?"

"Eyes front, soldier."

"Give me a break, dude. You're over there trying to kill me with your crab guts, the least you could do is let my eyes wander a bit."

"And isn't that exactly why you're divorced?"

"Right, and now I can do as I please."

Mike slams a half-ravaged crab leg into his metal bucket. "You don't even know, do you?"

"Know what?"

"How much that girl loved you."

"Melanie from ward—I mean, Melanie?"

"Yes, *Melanie from wardrobe*, Ford." He snatches up a brown paper napkin and angrily swipes at his juice-covered fingers. "I'm guessing you don't know she calls Toni once in a while."

"She does?"

"At least a couple times a month."

That's unanticipated, enough to stun me into silence, and I don't respond right away. Over by the bar, I watch a young boy and girl, teenagers in love it seems, giggling next to the old-fashioned jukebox. He slips a coin into the slot, pushes a button, and the speakers immediately begin gagging on the early '90s sensation, Boyz II Men. Even the girl can't handle the syrupy sweetness because she teasingly punches him in the shoulder, shakes her head like she absolutely can*not* believe he picked that song to play, and marches off with her arms crossed, feigning embarrassment. The boy comes up behind her, tickles her, and they scamper back to their table. Young. In love. Clueless.

How godawful disgustingly appropriate, too, and just another sign that the universe is out there pointing and laughing. The first night I took Melanie out, post after-party once we finished wrapping an international shoot in Prague, the discothèque we visited played nothing but Boyz II Men. All. Night. Long. On repeat.

I ask Mike, "Why would she call Toni?"

"They're talking about their cycles."

"Really?"

"No, moron, why do you think? She calls to check on you, as if I have anything to do with where you put your dick or which city you're terrorizing on a weekly basis."

"What? Why would she call Toni for that? Doesn't make any sense. I haven't seen or talked to either of you in over two years."

"I know how long it's been. Let me rephrase. Toni says that Melanie calls to shoot the breeze and catch up, but it always feels like she's somehow trying to work you into the conversation. Like no matter what they're talking about, Melanie will eventually get around to saying something like, 'Oh, speaking of the Moose Lodge, has Mike talked to Ford lately?'"

"But *why* would she do that? We talk fairly regularly. Not about anything important, just quick how-are-you type stuff."

"And you tell her how you're doing?"

I nod and mumble into my beer.

"What?"

"I said, kinda, but not really."

"And that's the thing. Toni's guess is, Melanie, she sounds like she's hoping we'll reconnect."

"You and me?"

"You and me."

"Why?"

"Because, Ford, she thinks I'm good for you. Am. Or *was*. Who knows? She knows that Toni has no idea what's going on with you, and she knows that Toni would probably pour gas on your dick if you were pissing fire—"

"Ouch."

"Yeah, ouch. Mel . . . she's planting seeds."

Caribou arrives at the table and asks Mike if he would like more crab legs since it's Bottomless Crab Leg night, which is total bullcrap because crab legs are too expensive to be bottomless anything. It's quick proof that she, and probably the manager, are former fans of the show, and they're being nice to the has-beens. Mike says he's good, then Caribou asks me if I need anything else. The look of disappointment on her face—when she sees that I've yet to open the sandwich that she so accommodatingly retrieved for me—is enough for me to thank her and pry it open. She's gone before I can look up again, and on the inside flap, I find the prize inside: her cell number, a smiley face, and a heart over the letter *i* in her name.

I fold it over before Mike can see.

"Aren't you going to eat that?"

"Later," I tell him. "But, man, I'm deliberately not being obtuse, honest to God, but why in the hell is Melanie 'planting seeds' or whatever it is you think she's doing? I don't get it."

Mike drains the last of his Budweiser and leans up on his elbows. He belches, pauses, and pinches the bridge of his nose. "The only thing I can think of is, if she can get Toni to corral me into making amends with you, and maybe we hang out again, then that'll be good for, I don't know, future possibilities."

"What fucking future possibilities, Mike?"

"You. Her. The two of you, dipshit."

This punches me in the chest with about the same force as when the right-hander lifted Mike off his feet back at the Craghorn house. Only in a good way.

I think.

There won't be any demonic handprints left on my skin, but it hits equally as hard.

I had been holding out the tiniest bit of hope, and on occasion, had considered begging to atone for my sins, but I thought I'd have a better chance bringing some of my dead counterparts back to life.

"Melanie wants me back?"

Mike closes his eyes, lifts one corner of his mouth, and gives me a bemused, "Beats the hell out of me. I wouldn't have the slightest idea why."

"Going through you is just—"

"Ford," Mike says, stopping my blathering. "I have no clue, bro. She's obviously not going to come right out and say it to your face. You cheated on her. Many, many times."

"Six," I remind him.

"Whatever. You absolutely shredded her heart, and she can't come around asking you to try again because how pathetic would that be? No way, no how. She's not going to give up that kind of power, and, by taking the long road of, you know, trying to get us hanging out again, maybe it'll get you on the straight and narrow. You'll see how much of an idiot you were, and you'll approach her. It's the long con. She's got nothing to lose."

"That's . . ."

"Sneaky?"

"I was going to say risky. What if I didn't bite?"

"How the hell should I know? She probably would've found a different way."

My stomach is growling, yet I'm too dumbfounded to eat this hoagie. I ask Mike, "Did you figure all this out just by Melanie calling Toni and asking about me?"

"Pffffft," Mike scoffs. "Me? Fuck no. Toni said so."

"So the woman who would pour gas on my dick if I was pissing fire, your peach of a wife, she told you to come see me and tell me that my ex-wife is using this elaborate ruse to win me back?"

"Toni? Please."

"Melanie?"

"Nope."

"Then will you tell me what's going on? Enough with the twenty questions."

"I told you. I'm here to help Craghorn. That other stuff about Melanie, that's just B-roll footage. Side story. So there's that, and then there's this other thing." Mike stops Caribou as she's passing by with the remnants of someone's mangled crab. He orders two more beers, and once she winks at me and leaves, he says, "There's an offer on the table. A big one."

# CHAPTER 15

## CHELSEA HOPPER
### TWO YEARS AGO
### A Very Special Live Halloween Episode

"You're so brave," I told Chelsea as she climbed the ladder into the attic. It's amazing how often kids are absolutely fearless unless they're taught to be afraid or something happens that dissuades any further attempts at exploring certain areas of life. Case in point, I haven't touched tequila since I took a sip of my dad's back when I was eight.

Chelsea was five. Her birthday was three weeks earlier.

The colossal fiend hiding in the space above her head had been growing in strength for thousands of years.

What in the fuck was I doing?

I reached for her on instinct, wanting to change my mind, wanting to pull her back. Then I played it off as if I was trying to steady her. Goddamn it. I was a seesaw.

She could do it. I had to *believe* with everything I had that she could. Chelsea would win and the beast would return to hell where it belonged, and she would live a long, happy life. She would be free of the black clouds because she defeated the dark man. On her own. Like a big girl.

Chelsea paused on the third step up and looked over her shoulder at me, both hands with a white-knuckled grip on the ladder. "Mr. Ford?" she said in a whimper.

"Yeah, sweetie?"

"I'm scared."

"It's okay. I'll be right here. It's your fight, your bully, honey. You beat that bully up there, and you'll never ever have to be afraid again. You'll be *so* strong, and you can fight for the other kids who are scared."

Off camera, Mike said, "For God's sake, Ford, it's not like she's getting on a roller coaster."

I couldn't hear him in my earpiece, only in my free ear. Carla must have cut the feed to his live mic. It was probably a smart decision on her part. It might have been her only one during the entire scenario.

Chelsea said, "Will you come with me, Mr. Ford? Come fight the dark man?"

"I'll be right behind you, Chelsea," I told her, but— and like the giant asshole I was—I had already decided to hang back for the sake of good television. The ratings would launch outside the stratosphere. Some cosmonaut up on the ISS would be able to reach out the window and touch the chart's arrow as it sailed by on the way to the moon.

Some time ago, Mike told me I was getting dangerously close to letting the show, the sponsors, and the money go to my head. Said it was affecting my clarity of thought, and he was sure that I wasn't the same person anymore.

Of course I wasn't.

Back when we first started, I was some goofball with a camera and a few drunken cheerleaders, who happened to get lucky by capturing a life-defining moment on film.

Fast forward to last week where I sat next to Jennifer Aniston and told a couple of funny stories to David Letterman.

I wasn't the same person, but, yeah, when Chelsea paused on the fifth step, with her legs visibly trembling and her head not yet inside the attic access above, I could see how maybe all of this had gone to my head.

What was *wrong* with me?

One minute I was standing there actually thinking that this was good for Chelsea, that she would come out of that attic as a victor who would be able to face down anything. The next minute I was waffling—my heart was melting. I was an idiot. A beat later, I'd be right back to drooling over ratings and—

"I want my mommy and daddy," Chelsea said.

I gently squeezed her ankle to encourage her. "You can do this, Chelsea. Remember how I said that if you beat the dark man, you'll never have to be afraid again?"

"Yeah." There was a quivering lip behind that single syllable.

"You, Chelsea, *you* are the monster. The dark man is afraid of *you*. Now get up there and kick his—"

"Ford! Stop it, now!" I felt a strong hand on my forearm, fingers digging into my skin, yanking me to the side. It was Mike, pulling me away, trying to get to her.

"What're you doing?"

"Get her down from there. If you don't, I will."

"Mike—" I held up an index finger to the camera. "Always nice to see on live television, folks. Anything can happen. One second, please, if you don't mind."

In my earpiece, I heard Carla whispering. "That's good, that's good. Go with it. Live TV, Ford."

Mike said, "I'm getting her out of here. We can't do this!"

Carla whispered in my earpiece, "Take him out, Ford."

"What?"

"You heard me."

Mike was reaching up for Chelsea's legs when I yanked his shoulders, spun him to the side, and sent him to the floor with an abrupt leg sweep. He cursed when he cracked his head against a dark black chest with metal bindings, and rolled over, clutching his skull.

"Chelsea, you can do this. Don't listen to Mr. Mike, okay? Don't forget, it's afraid of *you*."

Liar, liar, pants on fire because they'll be burning in hell.

"Promise?"

"Absolutely."

Downstairs, the front door slammed open, followed by angry shouts from some of the crew and the distraught voices of Rob and Leila Hopper. I was actually surprised it had taken them so long to get inside.

I found out later, much, much later, that Carla had hired security and two brutes about the size of Hulk Hogan were blocking the front door. From the moment Chelsea said, "I'm scared," the sentries had been holding the

Hoppers back. It took a hidden can of mace for them to gain access.

Chelsea didn't understand what the sounds meant. Instead, she took the angry shouts to mean that she'd done something wrong, that she was in trouble, and she said, "I'm sorry, I'm sorry. I'll go!" She crawled up the last three rungs and disappeared into the gaping maw of the attic.

Downstairs, her parents screamed her name.

Mike, groggy from knocking his head, tried to get to his feet.

I looked at Carla. With every bit of sincerity, and no pun intended whatsoever, the malevolent smile slicing across her face was absolutely *haunting*.

Through the commotion, I heard Chelsea's footsteps as she cautiously crept across the attic floor.

And then it happened.

A deep, raspy growl, made of ashes and rage, poured out of the hole above us. I smelled sulfur and rot.

Chelsea shrieked and went silent, then a second later, she tumbled out of the attic, flailing head over heels along the ladder. I lunged and caught her before she hit too hard, but the damage was already done.

Overhead, I watched a black mass, darker than the lightless attic, as it hovered there. It seemed to be mocking me, taunting me, enjoying the spoils of its effort, and then it slowly slithered back inside.

Chelsea's eyes were half-open, yet she stared at nothing.

I turned to the cameras, ashamed and horrified at what I'd done. The wavering scale of my emotions tilted back to

145

the same caring human I had been ages ago, and I felt the softball-size lump clogging my throat.

*What have I done, what have I done, what have I done?*

The twenty-four-hour news channels, the nighttime talk shows, the tabloids, Facebook and Twitter, none of them used *this* image of me, so distraught and worried about that damaged angel in my arms, hating myself. No. They didn't use it at all, because to them, I was an awful, vicious, bloodthirsty devil, and I deserved the public castration of my character.

I had good intentions, though, didn't I?

Chelsea's eyelids fluttered.

I shouted at Carla, at Don the cameraman, at anyone who would listen to me: "Cut the feed. Cut the feed, goddamn it!"

Carla fired back. "No, Ford, we are staying with this!" It was unconventional for her, as a producer, to insert herself into the live television situation, but by then, it was obvious that she didn't care.

The Hoppers breached the second floor, and I moved for them.

Don, thank God, said something to Carla and lowered his camera. Even in the dim light surrounding us, barely a hint of it coming from some far off bathroom nightlight that we forgot to unplug, I saw that Don's cheeks were wet with regret.

Carla tried to block me, and I leaned into her with a strong shoulder. I was a runaway train. She was a cow on the tracks. She had no chance at stopping me. A breathy *oooph* flew out of her mouth as she careened backward, slamming into the wall. A picture frame fell and glass shattered around everyone's feet.

Rob reached us first. Leila was blubbering, bawling, and wailing her daughter's name. He took Chelsea's limp body out of my arms and handed her to his wife. Then he whipped around and nailed me with a bare-knuckled backhand across my right cheekbone.

I dropped. My face immediately puffed with fluid and split where his rigid knuckles had met skin and bone, blood trickling down while I struggled to get back up, eyes watery. It wasn't the first time I had ever been punched by a client, but it was the first time I absolutely deserved what I got.

My profuse apologies went unheard over Leila's horrified voice as Rob flicked on a hallway light. Deep, red, furious gashes arced across Chelsea's cheek, neck, and collarbone.

Three of them. A mockery of the Holy Trinity.

I couldn't help myself. I moved to the small family that had been through so much. I wanted to hug them. I wanted to apologize for a hundred years and tell them I understood that what I had done was wrong, that Carla Hancock influenced me, that I had been driven by greed and ambition, by my own stupidity. I wanted to beg their forgiveness for getting caught up in the moment, for convincing them that having Chelsea battle her demons would be a good thing.

I picked a fine fucking time to develop a conscience.

Blame the fog of war, or better yet, the fog of celebrity, but that was all bullshit. I knew better. I knew what I was doing. The catalyst was—the fulcrum to the whole state of affairs—was that I didn't stop myself, and I didn't stop Carla when I should have.

Mike was right all along. Mike was always right.

I thought about that as I bent down to the traumatized Hoppers. I put my hand on Leila's back, and she hissed, "Don't you touch me," with all the ferocity of that thing hiding in the space over our heads.

Before I was able to respond, I felt her husband's hand on my throat, grasping tightly. "Once wasn't enough?" he asked.

Through his grip crushing my windpipe, I croaked, "I'm sorr—" and then his fist centered my nose. I heard the sharp crack as the bone shattered, and then I was falling, landing on my back, choking on the blood gushing down my throat and into my open mouth.

The room flashed whiter than the hallway bulb, and I realized it wasn't my vision reacting to the blow.

I rubbed my eyes, trying to see what happened. Was it a ball of energy? Was the creature upstairs manifesting, gathering strength to attack again?

No. It was Carla, chuckling, thumbing furiously on her phone.

"You're such a dick," I said, groaning, rolling onto my knees. Behind me, the Hoppers thundered down the stairs to the first floor. "What's—"

"That's an amazing picture, Ford. So much blood. I'm thinking CNN, MSNBC. Lead story everywhere."

"Don't."

"You'll be fine," she said, without an ounce of sincerity or concern in her voice. "There's no such thing as bad publicity, right?"

# CHAPTER 16

Mike wants to wait until Caribou is back with the next round of beers before he explains what he means, because he feels like, in his own words, "This whole goddamn discussion needs to be numbed by more alcohol."

"I actually don't want another round," I tell him. "Not a good idea to investigate with too much of a buzz, remember? Or are you planning on ditching me?"

Mike wobbles his head as if this is something he considered. "The thought crossed my mind, but no, not after what happened back there."

I'm fairly certain that Caribou gets the beers to us in record speed, because hey, we're the washed-up superheroes from *Graveyard: Classified*, yet I'm so zoned in on Mike's revelation that I forget to thank her, and I also forget to take another glance at that perfectly cupped rear. Good on me, I guess.

"So, about this offer. You're here to, what, *pitch* me? Were you planning to do this anyway? Like, what if I hadn't called you today, then what?"

"Ease up, cowboy. I'm getting there." He takes a long pull from his bottle of Budweiser. "The short and dirty is, Carla Hancock has some interested parties. People have been keeping tabs on you."

"*Carla*? Not a chance in hell," I say, and I'm already on my way up from the seat.

Mike pats the air, motioning for me to sit down. "Chill for a minute. Hear me out. She's got an idea for a project, and based on the feedback she's been getting—I kind of agree. I think it could be huge."

I sit, but I'm not happy about it. "Just who are these 'interested parties,' Mike?" I make sure to emphasize the air quotes around 'interested parties' and then follow that up with a quick wave to a younger boy at the next table. He's definitely interested in me. "Who's been keeping tabs?"

Mike looks confused, like I just told him that water wasn't wet. "Have you not been on the Internet lately?"

"Nope." And that's the damn truth. After the incident with Chelsea, after Wolf Blitzer, Brian Williams, Jon Stewart, and all the rest of those guys completely eviscerated me, after my sneering face was plastered all over the Internet, after the lawsuits, after everything shitty about those six months, post-live-show trauma, I needed to walk away.

"Seriously?"

"I have a phone. It rings. I have a website with my contact information so stumped detectives can get in touch. I answer e-mail from my mom and dad. I haven't tweeted, or posted, or blogged, or so much as surfed for porn in about a year and a half, so no, I haven't been on the Internet lately."

"*Really?*"

"Why is that so hard to believe?"

"Well, I mean, I figured that Captain Ego had to *look*, you know? Had to see what people were saying about him."

I have to admit, I'm curious, but after my righteous defiance just then, I most definitely can't go begging for him to tell me what's been going on in the world of social media. I make some offhanded joke about being on the psychiatrist's orders to stay away from mentally damaging material—which, honestly, isn't much of a joke.

"Folks are out there watching, Ford."

"*Again*, who are these people and what are they watching?"

"Anybody and everybody. Former fans. People like to keep up, you know? Nothing is private or personal anymore. And it's simple things, too, like hypothetically, maybe some detective took a selfie with you in Anchorage six months ago, he posts it online somewhere, some picture of you smiling and giving a thumbs up while he's got his arm around you; that thing gets a thousand likes and your name lives on. Fans get to see that the almighty Ford Atticus Ford didn't let a little bad press get him down. Some of the crazies have online maps tracking your trips."

Now it's my turn to say, "Really?"

"You still got murdered publicly for about two weeks after the lawsuits were tied up, but then they found that senator from Oklahoma with four hookers in his office and poof, you're old news. It's amazing how fast people move on."

I sip my beer. Time for a little revelation of my own. "Glad I'm no longer the social pariah—thank God—but the good thing is, I've been perfectly happy away from all that. At least for the time being. But there's always been this thing, this idea—never mind."

"What?"

I can hear myself saying it out loud, and the thought sounds insane. "I've been thinking about pitching another show when I'm ready. Maybe a show where a crew follows me around and I help these detectives solve crimes, like I'm out there doing good for society."

"Redemption."

"It's more like I'm looking at the world as a good place that I can help, but yeah, you could say redemption is a factor. I've made a couple of phone calls. Mostly it's been wishes and wants or ifs and buts." I have to take a sip of this beer. My throat has gotten dry. It's the first time I've admitted this to anyone other than Ulie.

The bottle clunks against the table, half of it gone.

Apparently I needed more than a sip.

"Could work," Mike says, "but listen to this. Since you're not public enemy number one anymore, Carla has an even bigger idea."

I haven't talked to Carla since our last day in court when the judge ordered The Paranormal Channel and its subsidiaries to pay the Hoppers 6.66 million dollars in damages.

I shit you not: 6-6-6.

Maybe Judge Karen Dunham had a sense of humor. Maybe she was trying to send a message.

Regardless, Carla tried to shake my hand, I flipped her the bird instead, and I haven't seen nor heard from her since.

"Carla has an idea," I say, "and I don't fucking care."

154

Mike puts his elbows on the table and leans toward me. "I completely agree."

"You do?"

"Yeah, fuck Carla. But . . ."

"Why did I know there was a 'but' coming?"

"You're hoping for redemption, yeah? Here's Carla's proposal: we make a documentary, hour and a half long, give or take, and she thinks she can get *national* theatrical distribution. The great Ford Atticus Ford is coming to a silver screen near you." He makes a wide gesture with his hands, displaying my name up on some invisible marquee. "We're talking in the neighborhood of fifteen hundred theaters on opening night. They've conducted interviews with focus groups and the tests have scored astronomically. Carla thinks she can finagle us some points on the back end, too. Ford, don't shake your head. Listen to me. We're talking tens of *millions* of dollars. All we'd have to do is spend a couple of weeks shooting, and if it does as well as they project, we'd be set for life."

I can't help but get titillated by the suggestion. My brain is buzzing with a hundred concepts already. There have been so many cases that I've worked on in the past two years that could use national attention. Hate crimes, domestic abuse, child abandonment—so many charities and organizations that need better funding and resources.

I'm not worried about the money. Regardless of what happened with the show, I walked away with plenty in my coffers. So did Mike, I thought.

"Let me think about it," I tell him, keeping my bubbling enthusiasm buried for now. "And I'll think about it on one condition. You keep Carla as far away from me as you possibly can."

Mike grins and lifts his finger to Caribou, ordering another round. "Carla suspected that would be the case, and she's already agreed to take a hands-off production credit to get you on board. You're the talent, Ford, the draw, and she knows that. I know it, too. You're the face, I'm the brains."

I don't even know how to express myself, so I hold up a saltshaker like it's a glass of champagne. "I'm not saying yes, mind you, but man, this is unreal. It's exactly what I've been wanting for almost two years now. There are so many things we can do. Wait, yeah, there's that lighthouse down in Florida. I got in good with the chief of police there—I'm sure he would love to have us work on this impossible cold case they've been looking at since 1987, and I know he—"

"Ford—"

"—would be totally cool with loaning us one of his detectives—"

"—Ford—"

"—for a couple of weeks—"

"Hey. Dude. Listen to me. We aren't going to have creative control."

My heart slams to a stop like a crash test dummy's head against a steering wheel, then sinks down to somewhere around my colon. "We don't?"

"No, they already have the concept worked up. It's the *concept* that tested so goddamn amazing."

"Which is what?"

"We go after the right-hander that hurt Chelsea. We fight back."

I'm flabbergasted that he would even suggest such a thing, let alone be on board with it. After all we went through with that family. After everything we put that little girl through. "Mike. *Mike*? You're kidding, right?" I ask this around a flabbergasted chuckle.

"It's what the people want."

"No. No, no, no. Not a fucking chance. I am not putting Chelsea Hopper through anything else. Not publicly. Never again. I can't even think of all the ways I would say no to this. And even if, by some miracle of the heavens above that I would give five seconds of thought to the possibility, the Hoppers wouldn't come within a thousand miles of me. They would rather drive a wooden stake through my heart than see my face again. Are you nuts? Is Carla nuts? What the hell?"

He scratches his forehead with the mouth of the beer bottle. "You finished?"

"I'm just getting started."

"Before you do, hear me out."

I remain silent, fuming.

Mike continues, "I don't know how she did it. Probably because she's some magical sorceress and sold the souls of a million newborns to the devil himself, but Carla got the Hoppers to agree."

"What!"

"In concept alone, nothing more. They don't want anything to do with the story, or the filming, or the production. The marketing, the celebrities, nothing. They're only granting the rights to their family's story—*because*—they have a memoir coming out this fall. They—"

"So now *they're* exploiting Chelsea? What happened to all the money they got in the settlement?"

"After all the lawyer fees and suits and countersuits and appeals, they didn't come away with all that much. Haven't you kept up with this?"

"Obviously not."

"It's how it works, Ford, you know that. That being the case, if somebody from Fifth Avenue, or wherever those big publishers live, somebody shows up on your front doorstep with a check that has two commas and six zeroes in it, and you don't have to fight anybody in *court* for it—it's easy to see how some small, tortured family like the Hoppers might hand over the rights for a bigger house, maybe a deeper college fund for Chelsea. Cosmetic surgery to conceal the scars that a fucking *demon* gave their daughter? You'd do the same, right?"

From my position, having had money, and having kept money, enough to last me for a long, long while, my answer is no. It's not worth it. However, given what I know about the Hoppers and their situation, okay, yeah. Maybe it's not necessarily exploitation if they feel like their story could serve as a warning to other families looking to cash in.

Hell if I know. People do strange things to fatten their bank accounts.

I ask Mike, "So they're on board with this whole fucked-all-to-hell idea as long as a paycheck is involved, and they don't have to look us in the eye?"

He salutes me with his beer bottle.

158

"And you're okay with this? You're okay coming back? Honest to God, Mike, I never thought I'd hear from you again. I called you today because I needed help, like actual, legitimate help with this badass right-hander because there's no other person on this planet that I would trust to go to war with me against something so strong, and then you show up, lying about how you just want to help Craghorn—"

"I'm not lying about that. He needs help, for sure."

"Then you drop this on me? What in the immortal fuck, dude? Do you need the money? What's the deal? Why the flip-flop? One minute you're punching me in the face and the next, you're practically begging me to come work with you again. I—I can't even fathom what's going on here."

Mike snorts and looks away; he can barely make eye contact with me. "The truth is, it took a few trips to a shrink, but I finally got around to forgiving you. And, for months now, I've been waffling about whether I was actually going to say something. I was there, man. I totally was. And then—then I showed up today, saw your face, and a whole rush of anger came on like goddamn Niagara Falls and I couldn't let it go again. Not until, well, not until we got back into the groove. By then it was just—this is hard, dude. Man to man, this opening-up thing. The doc says I gotta do it, though. Good for my head." He tips back in his chair, nibbles on his bottom lip awhile before he continues. "So there's that. And then, Toni and I, we got caught up in some bad investments," he adds, like he's already regretting the words coming out of his mouth.

"You? Captain Penny-Pincher?"

"I was stupid. Impulsive. Greedy, with a wife that wants nice things. I don't know how much cash you have left—"

"Plenty."

"You would've thought I had rocks up here," he says, rapping his knuckles against his skull. "I had all these people coming to me with 'investment opportunities,' and shit. There was this one with a salsa factory down in Guadalajara. Profit margins were supposed to be—you know what, it doesn't matter. The money went first, then the houses, the cars. The kids are so ashamed of me, they've barely spoken to me in months. We managed to keep the beach house in Kitty Hawk, but that was because we took every single penny we found to save it. I'm talking, like, Toni and I were smashing the kids' piggy banks with a ball-peen hammer. It's been tough, bro, I won't lie. I've tried to get my own ideas made into shows, checking around with all the old contacts, ringing them up. They wouldn't touch any of my pitches, not without you. Not without the almighty Ford Atticus Ford running point. I was so pissed that I didn't even want to look you in the eye, much less be on another show with you ever again. It took a while, but I got over it."

"But why now? Why this thing with Carla and the Hoppers?"

His shoulders go up to his ears and then drop, resigned. "Same goes for me. Like I said, somebody comes at you with promises of a check that has six zeroes and two commas, it's hard to say no. I'm not proud of it."

I take a second to let this marinate. Mike's broke; he obviously and desperately needs the money, so much so that he's willing to overlook my past transgressions. He's also willing to overlook the fact that we would once again be allowing Carla Hancock to exploit the story of little Chelsea Hopper.

I want to tell him to go to hell, that I will *not* take advantage of her again, even if her parents are blinded by the dollar signs in their eyes.

But I could also get national attention for something I've been doing privately already with my own investigations. Millions of theatergoers could watch as I send that bastard right-hander back to where he belongs.

Talk about emotional wavering. I'm like a swing set in a hurricane.

Mike says, "I get it, Ford. It's a big whammy. You probably need some time. Just promise me you'll think it over, okay?"

Until I have a chance to process this, I refuse to tell him that I've already been working on Chelsea's case on the side.

"Let me sleep on it. But first you have to help me beat that thing over at Craghorn's. I have a job to do, and you owe me for the surprise punch in the nutsack."

# CHAPTER 17

Mike and I remain silent on the ride back over to Craghorn's house. He tossed his idea grenade in my direction, and he probably feels like he's allowing it to do the smart thing and simmer awhile before he brings it up again. The only thing he does say is this: "Kind of a dick move to spring it on you like that."

I agree with a simple, "Yeah."

Then we pull into Craghorn's driveway. With his car gone, and Detective Thomas's unmarked sedan out of the way, I'm thankful we don't have to spend fifteen minutes driving around the block, praying someone will leave a spot open.

We slam the doors of the rented Honda closed and stroll through the gentle sprinkle, turning and climbing the steps, side-by-side. In my mind, I'm picturing us as two gunslingers in the Old West, starring in an action movie directed by Michael Bay, where we're marching in slow motion with some badass guitar riff overlaid in the background.

We did that for an episode at some ghost town in Nevada back during season five, and I'm fairly certain it was my favorite thirty seconds of staged footage on the show.

I use Craghorn's spare key to unlock the deadbolt and then reach for the door handle. It's a chunk of ice. I picture my hand getting stuck to it, ripping off a layer of skin. Instinctively I recoil, and it's nice to see that I don't leave anything behind on the metal when my hand comes free. "Jesus, feel that."

Mike touches it with the back of his hand and whistles. "That's insane. How warm is it out here?"

"Eighty-five, at least. Can you imagine the strength of that thing inside?"

"I don't want to."

"And Louisa is trapped in there with it."

"Yup," Mike says, matter-of-factly. "Ready to rock?"

I can't quite tell if his enthusiasm is manufactured so he'll be on my good side as I ponder his offer, or if he's now legitimately excited about the investigation. My guess would be a mixture of both.

"Here goes." I reach for the doorknob again and turn it gradually. I don't know why I'm trying to be quiet. That bastard inside already knows we're here. He probably sensed us coming before we hit the 1500 block on this street.

The door, weighty on its hinges and off-balance, swings inside without my help, screeching as it goes, and my thoughts instantly go back to how well that sound would've played during an episode. We would've magnified it, placed a couple of layers over it and, presto, you've got this chill-inducing shriek that sets the mood and tone for the next hour.

Mike, ever the gentleman, motions inside and says, "After you."

I actually hang back for a moment. It's not often that I get legitimately scared, but whatever's inside here has the potential to do some major league damage to our souls, and I do something that I haven't done since we went into the Hopper house for the first time years ago.

I say the Lord's Prayer, loudly, raising my voice into the long, deep, dark entryway, as if I'm talking into a tunnel that leads straight to hell. I touch my crucifix necklace, which feels warm against my skin, and make the sign of the cross over my chest.

Mike joins me, and to any of the neighbors, anyone passing by, we must be a sight. Two grown men, praying *into* a house.

When the prayer is finished, I add, "Hear me now, demon. You have no dominion over my body, or the body of my friend, Mike Long. You have no right to my soul, or the soul of my friend. We are here under the protection of our Lord and Savior, Jesus Christ. Once we enter, you are not allowed to touch us. You are not allowed to harm us in any way. We are protected by Almighty God, and you will obey us and listen to our orders. We are here to ask questions. We are here for information. And, above all, we are here to free the soul of Louisa Craghorn, and we are here to demolish your control over her surviving husband, Dave Craghorn. Do you understand us? We are protected by our faith, we are here to take back this house, and we are here to wreck your fucking ass."

Mike chuckles. "Forever and ever. Amen."

"Let's do this."

Mike and I step across the threshold. We make it three steps inside, enough to clear the path of the swinging door, and it slams behind us, the powerful shock echoing throughout the house.

We barely have time to flinch and look behind us, hoping that it was the wind, before we hear a malicious, throaty growl coming from upstairs, which is followed by the thundering sound of footsteps stampeding down the stairs.

"What the—" Mike says, unable to finish his sentence, as we're both hammered in the chest and thrown into the corner where we fall limply like old jackets.

Mike moans and sits up, rubbing his rib cage and looking like he didn't make it off the canvas after the referee's ten-count. It takes me a second, too, because I feel like I'm breathing through water. With a hit like that, who knows what's going on inside my lungs, but I can't stop now. I can't back out and run away.

"Where'd it go?" Mike asks, whipping his head around as if he can spot the next impending attack.

I do the same. For the moment, the energy in the hallway feels different, as if we just experienced a paranormal Hiroshima, and the aftereffects of the atomic blast are settling down. "Gone, I think. Feels . . ."

"Lighter," Mike says. "You're right. Hit hard and fast, now it's gone."

"For the time being."

"Oh, it'll be back."

"Gonna be a take-no-prisoners kind of night."

166

Mike has managed to get to his feet, and he agrees with me as he clasps my forearm and pulls me up alongside him. He says, "Three guesses what's showing up on our skin right now, and the first two don't count."

"I'll show you mine if you show me yours?"

We both lift our shirts, and, as expected, we have wide, red splotches that are condensing to claw-tipped handprints. It looks as if Mike got the left and I got the right.

"Son of a bitch. That hurt." I'm still having trouble trying to get a full breath. I double over and wobble with my head cloudy and knees weak. I count to twenty with my eyes closed, inhaling and exhaling in a steady rhythm, and when I look up, Mike is gone.

It's a weird thing, this sensation I'm feeling, because at once I'm feeling abandoned—that childlike fear of being left alone, away from my mother—and terrified of the remote possibility that our enemy has snatched Mike out of thin air.

But rather than Mike having experienced some sort of paranormal rapture, he rounds the corner from the living room, snapping his equipment belt with one hand and handing me his GS-5000 with the other. I take it from him and enjoy the comfortable bulk in my hands. It's almost like a security blanket to me. If I can communicate with what's on the other side, I'll know whether it's an entity that I can approach, or something that requires extra protection from the Big Man upstairs. Whether it was birthed from human loins or the fires of Hades, it's essential to know what's there.

167

Mike opens a bottle of water, and instead of sipping it, he sniffs at the opening. He scrunches his nose and asks, "Does holy water go stale?"

"What?"

"I mean, does the blessing wear off?"

"I doubt it."

"Good, because I've had this same stuff since that episode in Missouri, the one where we thought that right-hander was terrorizing the family of clowns. Remember?"

"Yeah, what a disappointment."

As it turns out, our entire crew, producers and all, were thoroughly duped by the Morgansterns, who just happened to be a family of professional clowns hoping to gain more exposure for their entertainment company. Lesson learned.

I ask Mike what our plan of attack is.

"Beats me. This is your gig, Ford. I'm just along for moral support."

I feel a cool rush of wind crawl across my exposed skin—my arms, hands, neck, and cheeks—and I know that there aren't any open windows in the house. It's almost as if this demonic entity is caressing me. "Let's move," I tell him. "Feels like it's coming back for another round."

There's nowhere to hide, of course, and I'd rather be in action than simply standing in front of the firing squad, waiting on demonic possession bullets to come flying at my head.

We coordinate our efforts around the living room, kitchen, and hallway, checking each of our spotcams. They're still working, and while I would love to spend an hour or two scanning through them to see if they picked up evidence while we were out for dinner, we don't have the downtime that we would on a normal investigation.

Mike and I, we're in an active, live-fire situation, and the enemy isn't going to sit back while we hunt for proof of his existence.

Mike says, "I don't know why, man, but I feel like this goddamn thing retreated upstairs. I feel safer down here, though."

"While the answers we *want* are upstairs."

My hands are sweaty. I wipe them on the legs of my slacks. Mike used to chide me about how my hands got wetter than a dog's tongue the first few times we filmed. It's not an easy thing, being entertaining.

Mike sees me swiping my palms and grants me a pass, because a second later he's doing the same thing. I tell him, "Here's the plan. We don't need to bother with EMF sweeps or anything generic. That's just telling a zebra he has stripes. We head up and jump immediately into the DVR. We'll do a few sprint sessions to see if we can come up with a name."

"Works for me," Mike says.

There's power in a name, which is why we'll try to wrangle it out of this sucker.

He adds, "He's not gonna give it up easily. This ain't prom night where everybody's eager."

It occurs to me that we've been wasting too much time. "Shit, Mike. Let's move. Hurry, hurry." He's chasing me up the stairs, asking what the problem is, as we take them in leaps of twos and threes. "We should've been up here right away trying to talk to Louisa while that fucking thing charges up again."

Mike says, "*I'm* out of practice. *You* should have known better."

I let the jab go because it's the truth. Then again, I haven't faced anything this overwhelming since the Hopper house. I've spent the past two years tracking down murderers and victims in the afterlife, but nothing like this.

I start the digital voice recorder in my hand, pop the earbuds in, and say, "Louisa? Are you here? It's Ford and Mike. Do you remember us from earlier? We just want to ask you a few questions. And listen to me, Louisa, you don't have to be afraid of us, but you do have to be afraid of that thing when it comes back. It knows why we're here, it knows we want to give you peace, and as soon as it can, it's going to come for us, and for you. Can you tell me if you can hear my voice?"

We wait in relative silence. I hear nothing but the thin whisper of white noise humming through the minuscule speakers wedged in my ears.

The floorboards creak underneath Mike's feet, and I don't bother to mark it on the recording because, for the time being, I don't care about reviewing these tapes tomorrow. I'm not concerned about what I'll be doing in a week. I am focused on the now.

I want this fight to end before sunrise.

I want to have some solid evidence for Detective Thomas.

I want to walk out of here victorious, with the demon gone, Louisa drifting toward the light, and Dave able to enter his own home again, without fear of pain, possession, or more scratches marking his damaged skin.

Can we do it? Can we be successful?

Or are we a couple of ants trying to take down an elephant?

# CHAPTER 18

While we wait for Louisa to make contact, I go over the details of the day in my mind, and something from earlier pokes its head out at me.

"Mike?"

He mumbles, "Mmm hmm?" in response, focused on the thermal imager in his hand.

"Didn't you say there was something weird about the scratches all over Craghorn? Did it ever come to you? I was thinking about it just now, and—"

Mike says, "Hang on, I think I'm getting something here. Take a look at this. Down there at the end of the hall. You see it?"

I lean over to look at the small screen. Just like before, it's too cold in here to get an accurate reading with the rainbow version of the heat signatures, so Mike has it on the black-and-white setting. It's almost as bad, but better than nothing.

He points to a small white blob in the doorway of the western-facing guest room. "Right there. Doesn't that look like something is peeking out at us?"

"Um, maybe a head and—whoa!" The thing, whatever it was, darts back inside the room. "Move, move, move," I tell Mike, and we're darting down the hall, bravely running into battle. I won't say we're storming the beaches of

Normandy, because yeah, we're not facing down the German artillery, but this is still pretty damn scary. You drop onto those chilly beaches in France, take a bullet to the chest, and you're a goner. Here, in this house, if it's the demon we're running toward and not Louisa, either one of us could face a full-bore demonic possession and a lifetime of sitting in a padded cell, trying to gouge out our own eyeballs with that morning's gelatin spoon.

Give me a German bullet any day. I'll take the quick road home, thank you very much.

In hindsight, maybe we should've tiptoed to the door, but son of a bitch, I'm so amped and ready to kick some ass that I don't hold back, and neither does Mike. He's taken two direct hits from this thing, and I'm sure he's itching to do some waterboarding with holy water.

We jam our shoulders together as we try to get into the guest bedroom, and it's slightly comical. Three Stooges, Laurel and Hardy, Jerry Lewis—shit like that, and it's the kind of thing that Carla would've loved to add into an episode to show the viewing audience that, yes, indeed, we are also human. Goofy ones.

Mike wrenches his body to the side, and we fall through the doorway, stumbling into the open space. It's undisturbed. Nothing has been moved. It looks exactly the same as when Craghorn showed me earlier today when I first arrived with the detective. It used to be a guest room, now it serves as a storage space, cluttered with a few cardboard boxes sitting about, some storage containers with multicolored lids, a pile of women's clothes lying on the floor, still on hangers. My guess is, those belonged to

Louisa, and this empty room is as far as he made it with them.

The thing I notice right away is that there's the barest trace of a flowery smell in here.

It's a good sign.

Mike inhales deeply. "No demon farts. What is that? Roses?"

"Perfume, yeah. Anything on the therm?"

"Just the ambient room temp."

I hold up Mike's GS-5000, readjust my earbuds, and say, "Louisa? Was that you? Please don't be afraid. Do you remember us from earlier? This is Mike, and I'm Ford."

I've done this for more than a thousand investigations, but I will never get over the chills that creep up my arm when I hear a voice from beyond the grave.

Every. Single. Time.

*"I'm . . . here . . ."*

I quickly rap Mike on the shoulder. "I got her," I say, and then I offer him the right earbud. He plugs it into his left ear and leans closer. "There you are. Thank you, Louisa. Listen, this is important. We don't have much time. That thing—"

*" . . . demon . . ."*

It's a whisper from a thousand miles away, but it's right beside us, too. Distant, raspy, and full of fear.

"Yes, the demon. We're here to help you, so it's important that you listen to us."

*" . . . trapped . . ."*

"Mike," I say, nudging him. "Do you see her on the therm?"

He shakes his head, looks at me with a sharp squint, his mouth pinched, and frantically motions for me to keep talking to her.

"You're trapped, yes, and we want to free you. I absolutely promise that we're going to get you out of here, but in order to beat this thing, we need your help. We need a name, okay?" I slow down my words and make sure to enunciate. "Do you know its name?"

"... *name* ... *Azeraul* ..."

Mike asks me, "Did she say 'Azeraul'? I'm assuming that's the demon's name? Have you ever heard of that one before?"

"Doesn't sound familiar. Louisa? Are you still there?"

"... *here* ..."

"Thank you. We're proud of you, and I know it's going to be tough, but hang in there for a little bit. It won't be much longer."

Mike is panning the thermal imager around the room, trying to find any sign of our companion, and then he takes a quick look back down the hall. It's not like Azeraul would need to use the conventional methods to enter a space, but I can see how Mike would feel like it's a natural reaction.

"Ask her about the case," he says. "Ask while we have her on the line."

"It's too much. Not right now. Let's get that thing out of here and then—"

"Ford!" he barks. "We may not get that chance and you know it. She's using up so much energy already just to communicate. If this Azeraul bastard builds up enough energy for another attack, she could be too weak. This is it, bro. We gotta do it now."

"I don't want to put too much—"

Again, he barks, "Ford!"

"Okay, okay. Louisa, if you're still here, if you can still communicate, there's something else we can do for you. If you want to be at peace, if you want to go to the light, then tell us this: were you murdered?"

"... I ... was ... true ..."

"Can you tell us who did it? That's what we need to know, okay? If you want your soul to rest and finally leave this world behind, tell us now."

"... can't ... weak ..."

"Stay with us. It's okay, we're almost there."

"... demon ... here ..."

"No," I shout. "Don't go. Fight him. Fight it, Louisa. Give us the name of the person who murdered you. We're so close. Are you scared to tell the truth? Nothing can hurt you, I promise. It'll be fine. Give us a name and then go to the light."

Thinking that it may have been the mayor himself, and that he may have learned that she had kept a diary of their illicit affair and then threatened her, possibly even murdered her, I ask, "Was it the mayor? Did Mayor Gardner kill you? He's dead now. Died three years ago, and if it was him, I'm sure he's burning in hell. He can't reach you."

"... still love ... her ... go ..."

"No, no, stay. Please stay. We can do this together, I promise. I can protect you." I turn to Mike and order him to take out his holy water. He complies and begins saying a prayer that I don't recognize as he splashes it around on the boxes, her pile of clothing, and the curtains.

The main bulk of the approaching thunderstorm that has been threatening Hampton Roads all evening hangs in the distance, as if Mother Nature herself is too scared to approach. Small sparkles of lightning illuminate the night from the west. I'm glad the storm is hanging back because we don't need another source of energy for Azeraul.

I ask her again, "Mayor Gardner. Was it him?"

"... *her* ..."

"Her? Her who?"

"... *Azeraul* ..."

"I—what? I don't understand. The demon is a female?"

"*No ... but light ... above ...*"

"It's not a male? You're not making much sense. Can you explain what you mean? Louisa? Louisa?" And then the tape is filled with unbearable, deafening silence. I inhale the deepest breath possible, because I swear it feels like I haven't taken in oxygen in fifteen minutes.

Mike yanks the second earbud out and slings it hard enough to pull the other one out of mine. "Son of a fucking bitch," he snaps. "We *had* her. We could've solved this whole thing and been done with it, and then she tells us some crap about being in love with a demon? Are you kidding me? I mean, what is this bullshit? Something like Stockholm Syndrome?"

I put my hand on his shoulder. "Calm down. Mike. Hey. Breathe for a second."

"Bah," he grumbles, and shoves my arm away. He marches over to a window and leans up against it with his forehead, shoulders slumped, disappointed.

"You know as well as I do that we only get a small percentage of clear answers. That's how this works, and it's the same thing that I tell every single police department that I've worked with. You remember that. I know you do. You're not that far out of practice."

"Let me ask you this," he says, staring out into the night, his breath leaving small condensation circles on the glass. "How often are you *actually* able to help with an investigation, huh? How often do you come away with something tangible that they can use? Because, to me, it was always gibberish, the stuff we caught during a case, you know? At least the EVPs most of the time. When we captured apparitions on camera or saw a ball roll across the floor, that's what I could get behind. But the voices? I don't know how many times I wanted to tell you that you were full of shit, the way you tried to read between the lines and convince the audience that these random words we captured meant something. That's the part I never got, you know? Why do it? Why bother trying to force meaning onto nothing?"

"It's not nothing, Mike. It's *never* nothing. They're there. They're communicating."

"And you're making up stories around nonsensical crap."

"I'm trying to give these spirits an identity. They're people. Are. Were. Doesn't matter. They have a story and they're trying to tell it. Think of it like a coloring book. The

179

structure was there, it just needed filling in because that's what worked for the fans. And to answer your question, I give the detectives actionable material about forty percent of the time, honestly. At least according to my case records."

"That much, huh?"

"Yeah. You want, I can sit down with you and show you all my files."

"I believe you, Ford. It's just—"

"Just what?"

"This is going to come out of left field, but I *have* to know," he says, turning to me, crossing his arms. "Here's your chance."

"For?"

"I think, maybe—look, I can't think of a way to say it without getting all worked up—but fuck me, Ford, *why?* Why did you do that to Chelsea? Huh? Can you explain it to me? I can't even begin to tell you how goddamn let down I was. You were my brother. I thought I knew, man, and then . . . *that.* I don't get it. You already had money. You already had fame. Give me a reason, not an excuse. I never gave you a chance before, so tell me now."

I sidestep over to a rickety stack of crates, grunting an exhausted old-man groan, as I lower myself onto them. I'm tired. Emotionally wrecked on so many different levels. "Really," I say, tapping the digital voice recorder on my palm. "Really, truly, and honestly, I've been trying to figure that out for over two years now. Part of me got blinded by the moment, the potential to create, what? Television history? Who would've remembered it a year later other than our fans? The other part of me—on some delusional level—actually believed that if Chelsea was able to *literally* face down her demon, then she could take on the world."

"Oh, for God's sake, don't try to fool me or yourself with that horseshit. We didn't send her in there to come out with a *win*. She was a goddamn trigger object and you know it. We sent her in there to draw out that right-hander and get some good shots for Halloween."

"Nah." I shake my head. "That was me being 'TV Ford' around the producers and the network people. I thought I was doing the right thing. You and I, the crew, the producers, we'd all been through so many investigations together and we've all seen how horribly some families can get affected by the paranormal. Whether it's a pissed-off spirit or an actual demon, everyone knows that lives get ruined all the time. I can't even describe to you just how conflicted I was, but when I looked at Chelsea and her case, the ego was on one shoulder wearing the devil horns, carrying a pitchfork, and this overwhelming need to *help* her was on the other, wearing a halo and playing the harp."

Mike moves away from the window, steps over, and sits down beside me on the wooden crates. The slats creak under his added weight. "Fine, I get *that*. Here's what I don't get. Answer this, and we can drop it, okay? I'm so fucking tired of hating you for what you did. It's exhausting carrying around so much mental baggage. I'm not saying that we can bro hug and be done with it, but what I need to know is, why bring her back to that house after they'd managed to break free? That's the part I don't get. We could have done the show without her. They were twenty miles away, and she showed every indication of being fine. Happy little kid, back to normal. Why subject her to that house again?"

Here we go. I've been holding onto this for a long time. "Did I ever tell you that I went to see the Hoppers about a week before the investigation?"

"No." He shakes his head. "Wait, was that when you said you were taking Melanie to New York City for the weekend?"

"Yep."

"Why lie about that?"

"Because, I felt like, if I took you with me to do a *pre*-pre-interview, you'd squash the whole live show, and that's kinda why I went. I wanted to gauge the situation with the family and get some feedback before we went in, right? Like you said, Chelsea seemed fine. Seemed like a normal kid, and I thought that there wasn't any use in bringing her back."

"And?"

"And she *was* fine, great, wonderful, until she said—I'll never forget the chills I got—she said, 'If you go back to our old house, can you tell the dark man to stay out of my dreams?' That's when I knew. That's when it occurred to me that we had one helluva show on our hands and that she needed to beat it if she ever wanted calm in her life again. I've regretted the decision since she fell out of that attic. You don't need to hate me. I do enough of that to myself."

"Jesus," Mike says, holding out his right arm. "Look at my goosebumps."

"See what I mean?"

"No, not from that." He snatches an EMF detector off his tool belt, flips it on, and the meter immediately pegs in the red. "Azeraul is back. Get ready."

# CHAPTER 19

We used to do that sometimes—have deep, philosophical chats during the down periods. It never made it onto the show because who wants to see two paranormal investigators sitting around, having a heart-to-heart discussion? Nah, save that for the behind-the-scenes menu item whenever the box set of seasonal DVDs comes out. We both know that after a giant explosion of energy, like our attack downstairs, it can take some time for a spirit or a right-hander to recharge itself. Depending on the strength of the entity in question, it could be a couple of hours, or a couple of days.

Apparently, Azeraul needs about fifteen minutes to recover, which is just insane. We don't have any EMF pumps running, and that approaching storm has yet to move any closer. Sure, tiny droplets of rain pepper the windows, and the lightning flickers once in a while and illuminates the house, but it's not close enough for him to recharge his paranormal batteries.

Mike hops to his feet. He's thinking the same thing because he checks his watch and says, "That was just a little over fourteen minutes since the attack downstairs. Makes you wonder if that damn thing plugged itself into an outlet."

"Plan of attack? Stay put? Or, no, we should go back to that front room where we saw him earlier. Maybe Louisa was living in *here*, and he's playing house over *there*."

"Not that I think it matters, because he'll find us regardless, but I can tell you this much: dude is gonna be super pissed that his play-toy is gone. We could probably do a quick round to check, but it sounded to me like Louisa moved on."

"Definitely. She's gone," I say. "Just like always, and I don't know how I know, but I can feel it. Heaven or hell, she went somewhere else."

"Ssshh," Mike whispers, putting a finger up to his lips. "You hear that? Footsteps?"

"I thought it was a door latch. Metallic, maybe."

"Let's go check."

From down the hall, we hear a tremendous crash. Mike and I rush for the door, allow each other to exit without a comical mishap, and once we step into the upstairs hall, I can immediately tell what happened. In the far front room, the spartan one where Azeraul had hidden earlier, a rush of water is leaking out from underneath the closed door.

"The vase," I say.

"Yep."

"God, feel the temperature in here."

"Feels like it dropped another five."

"It must be fifty degrees."

Mike turns on his thermal imaging camera. "Good call. Solid forty-nine point two, except for that bedroom."

"What's it reading?"

He holds the camera sideways so that I can see the screen. The door is glowing white hot on the monochromatic setting. A small cursor, ironically in the shape of a cross, plots around the screen, scanning temperatures and giving us an idea of what the laser is picking up with various locations. When it dances across the door, I almost expect it to read sixty-six point six. Instead, I'm blown away when I see eighty-seven degrees.

"Eighty-seven? Are you kidding me? And that's the outside of the door."

"I can't even imagine what it's like inside there."

I feel a slight rumble in my feet. It's a muted shake, almost like the platform in a subway station when the train rolls in for a stop. "Dude? You feel that?"

"Yeah."

We both look down at the hardwood flooring and retreat a step, as if that will have any bearing on our safety.

"Any trains close by?" he asks.

"Nope."

"Didn't see headlights so I'm guessing no semis come down this street."

"Residential," I remind him. "No restaurants or convenience stores for blocks."

"Then it's our buddy, or not?"

"Azeraul? Could be, but I would think—"

Something pounds against the inside of the closed bedroom door.

*BOOM. BOOM. BOOM.*

It's thirty feet from us, but I can feel the reverberations in my feet. They've escalated. It's no longer the rumble of an approaching subway train. Instead, it almost feels as if we're standing on top of an unbalanced washer. Almost like a rhythmic thumping under the soles of our shoes.

To our left and right, here in this cramped hall, the walls are grumbling. I put my hand out and feel the pressure being built up inside them.

"This fucking thing is *strong*," I tell Mike. "Have you ever seen anything like it?"

"Not since the Hopper house."

It's dark in here. Damn, is it *dark*. You'd think with some of the streetlights outside, there would be more of a glow, yet it feels like Azeraul is draining all the light out of this place. No wonder Dave Craghorn had such a pallid look to his skin.

Craghorn.

Craghorn's skin.

I keep forgetting to talk to Mike about Craghorn's skin. No time for that now.

We both stand motionless, like breathing cadavers, watching the room, waiting on whatever comes next.

"Mike?" I whisper with a tremor in my tone.

"What?"

"I'm not gonna lie, dude. I'm not sure I want to go in that room." I expect him to shoehorn me into attacking this demon. I expect him to say something about how the great Ford Atticus Ford of the past would never back down, and what happened to wrecking this thing's ass?

Instead, he says, "Me—uh, me neither."

"Want to stall a minute, see if it burns itself out?"

"Please."

*BOOM. BOOM. BOOM.*

The pounding isn't just in the door this time, it feels as if a giant is slamming the home's foundation with a monstrous warhammer.

It's not enough to make me stumble, yet I have to hold my arms out to keep my balance. The hair on the back of my neck stands up. People always talk about how that happens to them during a scary movie—maybe it does, maybe it doesn't—but wait until you're standing in a house with a demon and see what happens.

That shit is real.

"I can't breathe. Can we get out of this hallway?" Mike asks without waiting for an answer. I agree immediately and follow him, albeit forward, which is not exactly my preferred direction, until we're at the landing where it's less suffocating. The long set of stairs stretch out below us, and we both move behind the banister to our right, as if these dark-stained slats will give us any layer of protection.

"How long do we wait?"

"As long as it takes. That door," Mike says, looking down at the thermal camera, "is up to ninety-two degrees. It *can't* sustain this much—"

A violent rumble interrupts Mike. The entire house shudders.

*BOOM. BOOM. BOOM.*

I tell Mike, "He keeps that up, he won't have much left."

"Seems like it's getting stronger. We gotta wait, Ford. I go home with company, especially something like this? Toni will murder me before *it* has a chance to."

189

"Agreed. I talk a big game, but this is an entirely different sport."

We're both so caught up in the moment that I realize we're not running any equipment other than Mike's thermal imager. We never had a chance to set up our spotcams on the second floor, and I still have the GS-5000 shoved in my back pocket. I'm hoping that our cameras downstairs are picking this up on audio and capturing the shaking.

I pull the voice recorder out, offer Mike an earbud, and he declines.

"Thanks, but I'd rather not hear what that thing has to say."

I press record and wait through the rumbling of the floorboards, the rattling of the picture frames, and the erratic breathing of one Mike Long, once famous paranormal investigator. Aside from the static hiss crawling in over the top of the surrounding noises, I hear nothing. I wait and I wait, and the floor continues to shiver under our feet.

*BOOM. BOOM. BOOM.*

I jump. Mike jumps.

And then we're engulfed in shuddering silence once again.

I expected demonic growls. I expected this almighty right-hander to come across the airwaves, shouting vicious words of putrid hate at us. But he's not, and after witnessing this display of incredible power, I'm not ashamed to admit that I'm *still* not going anywhere near that door.

"Can we take a breather for a sec?" I ask.

"Now?"

"I need to think about something else before I piss myself."

"Fair enough."

I ask him, "Probably not the best time, but Craghorn—what was it about his skin? Something made my sixth sense tingle."

"You're right, it is bad timing," Mike says, glancing at me while keeping a wary eye on the superheated bedroom door. "But yeah, what I didn't get was, if his whole damn body was covered in that roadmap of claw marks and scratches and scars, why weren't there any on his face?"

"There weren't?" I try to picture Craghorn in my mind—

*BOOM. BOOM. BOOM.*

Goddamn it.

—and I see a diminutive, timid man wearing slacks, a long-sleeve shirt, and a jacket in the middle of a summer heat wave. I haven't seen him in six hours, but under such duress with that fucking thing over there, trying to rip the house off its foundation, I'm having trouble recalling Craghorn's face. Long hair. Goatee. I picture him showing me his arms and his belly, his scarred back, and then his face comes into focus. It's somewhat pockmarked from an unfortunate childhood with either smallpox or acne, but not a single series of three claw marks mocking the Holy Trinity.

"Shit. Smooth as a baby's behind, wasn't it?"

"I wouldn't go that far."

"Fine, as smooth as the moon's surface, but what do you think it means?"

"Use your head, man—"

A gut-wrenching roar emanates from the room and scrapes at my eardrums. It's the wail of a million souls swallowing acid. It's a pterodactyl being burned alive. It's Godzilla stepping on a Lego in the middle of the night.

Mike puts a hand on my arm and pulls me into a retreating step.

"You don't think he was lying, do you?"

"That's exactly what I think."

"Craghorn was making it all up?"

"Well, not all of it. I mean, witness Exhibit A behind that door."

As if on cue, and reacting to us acknowledging his presence, Azeraul pounds the door yet again.

*BOOM. BOOM. BOOM.*

"Goddamn, that's getting annoying," Mike says.

"He's not backing down, is he?"

"EMF meter is red-lining big time."

"Okay, so, Craghorn. You think he's using this demon as an alibi? Sort of?"

"Think about it. He's got marks all over his whole body. Even told me they're on the bottom of his feet. While you were down talking to the detective, Craghorn showed me places I didn't necessarily want to see. He's covered. All but his face."

Lightbulb. Sometimes I'm dense. "Ooooh, which he can't hide in public with long sleeves or pants."

"Ding ding ding."

"So you think he killed her? You think he found out about Louisa's affair? Choked her to death, then dumped her in the Chesapeake Bay?"

"Doesn't that make sense to you?"

The pounding hasn't happened in at least thirty seconds, and I glance at the thermal imager to see if the temperature has gone down. Fingers crossed, I'm hoping Azeraul is burning himself out again.

Nope. The exterior temperature of the door has actually spiked by another degree.

"Ninety-three," Mike announces.

"I noticed."

"He's building up."

"I noticed that, too."

The doorknob begins to rattle. I can't see it from here, but I've heard that sound enough over the years to peg precisely what it is. It's a sound that's as distinct as clipping your nails.

"*Umm*," Mike whines, retreating another step.

I follow him.

"I'm buying that Craghorn is hiding something with the claw marks, but—"

"Ford?"

"I don't understand what it could be. Your theory makes sense from every angle—"

"Ford. Look."

"I see it." The door is creeping open, centimeter by centimeter. "But the thing is, Detective Thomas told me that Craghorn has a solid alibi. He wasn't anywhere near Louisa. He was out of town on business for two weeks prior to when they found her body. Forensics said she'd only been in the bay for a week."

"Hitman?"

The bedroom door slams open, violently. There's an explosion of plaster and the door gets stuck because the handle is imbedded in the wall.

We scamper back to Louisa's room. Why? Who knows? It feels safe back there. Going forward to reach the stairs would mean going *toward* Azeraul.

No, thank you.

The almighty Ford Atticus Ford and Mike "The Exterminator" Long are officially terrified.

Mike admits it out loud, and I'm not entirely sure I've ever felt this level of fear.

Now I know what little Chelsea Hopper must have felt like before I talked her into climbing that ladder.

I try to make a joke. I do that in the worst possible situations sometimes. It's a defense mechanism. I say, "Hey, Mike?"

"What?"

"Don't let the dark man get me, okay?"

# CHAPTER 20

You know what's really damn eerie? Looking down an empty hallway and hearing slow, methodical footsteps coming in your direction without being able to see what's there.

This isn't just my ego talking, but it's likely that I've performed more investigations than any other working paranormal investigator, in the public eye and out, yet that gets me every single time. You'd think I would be used to it by now. You'd think that I'd be like, "Oh, shucks, there's a spirit coming, time to go say howdy."

Nope.

Each time is different. Each new experience brings new fear, new challenges.

That thing marching down the hallway? It's an approaching storm, much like the flickering lightning and distant rumbles outside, and it's about to unleash the fury of hell instead of a cleansing rain.

I duck my head back inside Louisa's room. "He's coming."

"I can hear it."

"Not it. Him."

"Whatever the fuck that thing is, Ford, it's coming, and I can hear it."

Mike tells me this as he's frantically working with his digital voice recorder, the thermal imaging camera, the full-spectrum cameras, everything we brought, all of which seem to have simultaneously lost battery power. To a ghost or a demon, a fresh battery is a protein bar packed with extra caffeine.

Azeraul sounds like he's still twenty feet down the hall, and somehow he's reached inside this room and sucked the life out of our equipment, essentially leaving us defenseless.

Mike screams, "Shit!" and slams a now-useless recorder down onto a crate. A plastic button pops off, bounces to the side, and drops to the floor.

We exchange worried glances.

Worried about demonic possession. Worried about physical damage and pain.

Worried about taking something home with us that might affect our friends and loved ones.

For Mike, he has an entire family to worry about.

For me, it's just Ulie, but I love that mutt like my own child, and I don't want anything to happen to him. Pets are sensitive, I've explained that, but I've also seen horrible cases where family pets have been mutilated by outraged, jealous, vindictive spirits and soulless demonic entities as a means of retribution or mental torture. That's not happening to my pup. No way.

I'm filled with a renewed sense of vigor, thinking about this thing trying to do harm to our families.

They say that true courage is running into the battle even when you're scared.

Well, I'm no hero, but I'm not a pansy, either.

Mike shouts, "Goddamn it!" at the ceiling. "Another one, dead in *seconds*." He pulls a rechargeable battery out of a full-spectrum camera, flings it across the room, and we're immediately greeted with the sound of shattering glass. Just a picture frame. Not a window. Though I doubt Craghorn would care much if he's never coming back here.

In addition to the footsteps, Azeraul knocks on the wall.

Tap, tap, tap.

Step, step.

It sounds like hard-soled shoes on a hardwood floor, but I know better. That's the clop of hooves.

Step, step. Tap, tap, tap.

He's teasing us.

Step. Tap, tap, tap. Step.

"Holy water, Mike."

"What?"

"Your holy water. Give it to me."

He yanks the small bottle out of his utility belt and tosses it over. "That'll probably be like shooting charging bull with a marshmallow gun, but what the hell, you can try."

Step, step.

Tap, tap, tap.

"I can do this," I say. "You just see if you can get one of those DVRs working. Or the spirit box. Something. I want to have a chat with this son of a bitch."

"Yeah, right," he says, raising an eyebrow. "Don't do anything stupid. You know how you get when—"

I hold my palm up. "I got this. It'll be okay."

Step, step.

Tap, tap, tap.

Azeraul can't be more than ten feet from us.

Outside, over the rooftop of a distant office building, a bolt of lightning shreds the sky in half, a yellow streak across a mottled black canvas.

A beat later, thunder reverberates throughout the house, rattling loose-paned glass windows.

Sure, maybe that's a subtle warning from God, but the dude ain't here right now to tell me in person, so I'm pushing ahead.

I unscrew the cap on the bottle of holy water, shove it in my pocket, and then sidestep over to the bedroom door, scooting and sliding, really, until my shoulder is just inside the opening. I lean out quickly for a peek and duck back inside. It *appears* empty, as expected. For the sake of my soul, it's better that I don't see it. My morbid curiosity, though, would like to witness a demon manifest in the flesh. Once would be enough. Once might be the only chance I'd ever get.

Mike says, "Hey, hang on. Look what I found." He hands me a crucifix, a much larger version of the one hanging on the chain around my neck. "It was over there on top of that box. Must've been Louisa's."

"Little extra ammo never hurt anybody. You should probably know that you're in my will, just make sure the lawyers know where to find you," I say, and then take three quick breaths in succession. I dart through the doorway and hold the crucifix aloft with one hand, squeezing a short stream of holy water down the hall with the other. I manage to say, "In the name of our Lord—" before I hear the same eardrum-scraping scream as before.

Only now it's directly in front of me and so loud that I can feel the sound slithering over my skin.

Before I can react, before I can dart back into the room, a searing hot hand clasps my throat, clenching tightly, sharp claws gouging my skin.

I lash out with the crucifix, trying to use it as a hammer, and sling more holy water at the invisible demon in front of me.

Another acid-drenched screech fills the hall, and underneath it, I can hear Mike shouting, "Ford! Get back in here!"

The white-hot hand is crushing my windpipe. I manage to gurgle, "Can't. Too strong."

Another stream of holy water. Another wail.

"In . . . the name of . . . God, our Father in Heaven . . . I command you . . . Get off me!" I shove the crucifix forward, in the direction where I suspect Azeraul's face might be, and I hear the crackling, hissing sound of searing demon flesh.

A howling, louder than anything I've heard so far, explodes throughout the static-filled space around me. It's hideous and coated with such vile hatred that it weakens my heartbeat.

Then, a deep, disembodied voice says, "Hell waits for you, Ford."

And then the pressure on my neck is gone.

It hurts like, well, it hurts like hell, and I feel like someone held a hot iron to my throat, but at least I can take a breath.

It's warmer, too. Noticeably warmer, as if the temperature in the hallway is clicking up a degree with each tick-tock of the supposedly broken grandfather clock downstairs.

I slump to the floor. I barely have the energy to hold my head up.

My vision swims, and Mike is at my side, hands under my arms, trying to drag me back into the bedroom. He's saying something, yet I can't make out what, because the only thing that's at the forefront of my mind is that this demon called me out by name. Again.

There's power in a name.

$$***$$

I'm not sure how long I'm out, but it's the second time I've been unconscious around Mike today. At least it wasn't his fists of fury that put me down into la-la land. I'm hoping this doesn't become a trend, because I'm not a fan of it.

Actually, before I open my eyes, I lie here for a second because I can hear Mike talking, and it's slightly amusing. He obviously doesn't know I'm conscious yet, and this might be a perfect chance for good ammunition down the road.

"Dear Heavenly Father, hallowed by thy name, your will be done on earth as . . . As what? Jesus. Why can't I

remember this? On earth as in heaven! Right. That's right.
And then—shit. Forget it. Amen. Just do *not* let him be
possessed, okay? Please? I know you're up there, God, and
I know you're listening, because there can't be good
without evil and evil without good, and whatever that thing
was, it was evil, so I know you're up there, too. Just—look,
I'm sorry, okay? I'm sorry I didn't stick closer to my friend,
and I'm sorry I abandoned him, but you gotta
understand—it was harsh—*harsh*—that thing we did. *He*
did. And I couldn't stand by that, and now, Jesus, who
knows what's going on. All I'm trying to say is, if you'll take
this off of him, get this demon out of him, we can fight it,
and I'll make him, or we—*we*—can figure out what it was
that attacked the Hopper girl, okay? We'll fight it for you.
We'll be holy warriors, or whatever."

I open my eyes and say, "Dude, it's not your fault."

Mike yelps, lurches back, and then pulls me in with a
strong hug. He's overjoyed for a good fifteen seconds
before he leans into a solid punch that will certainly leave a
bruise on my chest.

"Damn you, Ford," Mike says. "How long were you
awake?"

"Lord's Prayer. After all these years, how it is possible
that you don't have it memorized?"

"You better believe I'm gonna learn it now. Are you
okay?" He helps me to my feet, hands on both of my
shoulders, and starts to survey me the way a mother does
when her only son gets home from the war.

"Does it seem brighter in here?"

I hadn't noticed that the storm finally arrived, but it's reached an apex. Lighting flashes and thunder bellows its damning curse. Bulging, pregnant drops of rain slam against the windows.

Yet the spare bedroom, our sanctuary, appears to be livelier. Alleviated. Unburdened.

"I swear, man, as soon as you got rid of that thing, it was almost like somebody turned on a low-watt lightbulb or lifted a blanket off the streetlights. So crazy."

Mike lets go of me and backs up a step with his hands on his hips. I roll my shoulders and crack my neck, then give him some bad news. "It's not completely gone," I say. "It's still here."

A grin spreads his lips, pulls his cheeks up until the dimples are on display—the same dimples that thousands of spotcamgirls tweeted and posted about for years. I haven't seen Mike smile like that since, well, it was a long time before Chelsea Hopper. I can remember that much.

"You're fucking with me, right?"

I'm not, and he knows it. We've been friends and partners long enough for him to understand what I'm getting at. I've mentioned that I'm 'sensitive' to spirits, for lack of a better word, and at the moment, I can feel that Azeraul remains in this house. Lurking. Holding back. Waiting and conserving his energy. If it's like before, it'll be another fifteen minutes or so before he can fully attack again.

I don't plan for us to be in this house for that long, but I'm not done yet.

"You can feel it, can't you?"

"He's weak, but he's here. I don't know where." I point to Mike's utility belt. Each of his devices hang in their slots like grenade duds, useless and weighing him down. "You got any batteries left for those?"

"Ford, no."

"Do you?"

"Yeah, one set left for the DVR. He didn't get those."

"Load 'em up."

"*Hell* no. Let's beat feet and get away from it. It's too powerful, and this is a fight we can*not* win. You *know* me, Ford. I don't ever back down from a challenge, but I know when to cut my losses and move on."

I hold out my hand and waggle my fingers. The international sign for "gimme."

"I'm telling you, don't do it. Don't risk it. Look at your neck. You're already contaminated. One more like that, and—"

"Mike! Enough. Just give me the damn DVR. You can leave if you want, but I need answers."

He relents with a huff forceful enough to knock down a Clydesdale.

"What?"

"Nothing, it's just that you remind me of somebody I used to know."

"Who?"

"The old Ford. The real one."

# CHAPTER 21

The upstairs seems dead—pardon the afterlife pun—so Mike and I move downstairs. He keeps checking his watch, every fifteen or twenty seconds, and I finally tell him to chill because the anxious repetition is driving my own angst level exponentially higher. "And besides," I tell him, "if this right-hander's recharge time is a little over fourteen minutes, then we have—"

"Eight minutes and thirty-seven seconds left," Mike says, interrupting with a voice that quakes over some obvious nervous tension.

"That's an eternity. If we were in the fourth quarter of an NFL game, we'd have, like, another thirty minutes to go."

"Shitty metaphor. We don't get any timeouts."

I smirk and see that my attempts at calming him aren't working. He's almost vibrating.

"You getting *any*thing on the live feed?" he asks.

"*Nada.* Quiet as a tomb in here."

"Are you intentionally fucking with me?"

"Probably a little." I readjust the earbuds, and if it's possible to physically do so, I listen harder. There's only the sound of our shoes on the hardwood floor, Mike's uneasy breathing, and the occasional creak of a board underfoot or a door swinging open. I don't bother audibly marking them on the recording because I'm so amped up about this moment, I'm mentally logging everything. It's only the two—well, three—of us inside this house, and the contamination from outside is so minimal it might as well not exist. We're in a vacuum, just us and him.

"Seven fifty," Mike informs me.

"Relax. *Please*."

"I can't, man." He cracks his knuckles and wiggles his fingers. "I don't know what to do with my hands when I'm not holding something."

"Use one of them to cover your mouth. I'm trying to listen. In fact, maybe I should go a little batshit on him, huh? Get crazy aggressive and try to draw him out before the timer stops."

"Are you nuts?"

"Rhetorical question? We draw him out before he's full strength, we get control of the situation, we get some answers, and we're gone. It'll be like we're psyching him out or something. Maybe demons are just like us. Maybe they get stupid when they're all worked up."

"Seven minutes, fifteen seconds. If you're going to do it, do it now."

"There's Big Mike. Back again."

"Whatever. *Go*. Do it."

Mike is basically going into this blindfolded and wearing earmuffs since I'm holding the last working piece of equipment. It has to be slightly unnerving to simply stand there and wait on the next attack to hit without any forewarning. So I understand his hesitation, but if I get what we need, it'll all be worth it.

"Azeraul!" I call out. "Demon child of Satan! How did it feel earlier when I kicked your ass with the power of God? Did you like that? Huh? Tell me. How'd it feel when a pissant, pathetic mortal like me gave you a nice little battle scar? All the other demons around the block, laughing at you, pointing at that nice crucifix branded on your forehead. I heard it, Azeraul. I heard the hiss. I heard your flesh searing with the burn of God's love. You're weaker than I thought. You're pitiful."

"Ford—"

"I got this."

"I'm just saying—"

"Azeraul. Are you there?" I hold up a wait-a-second finger to Mike when the distant sound of a child's laughter—a young girl—comes across the earbuds. I whisper to Mike, "Laughing. He's here. Taking the form of a girl."

"Oh, shit. Okay, okay, just be careful."

"I can hear you," I shout, slipping into the living room. The clock on the wall, a plain-faced one that maybe cost Craghorn a buck at a discount store, ticks with abandon, like it's projecting through a megaphone. "Come talk to me."

More giggling, followed by the angelic voice of a young child. She sounds like she might be about five years old, but I'm not fooled. I *know* this is Azeraul. I've been doing this awhile, and there's not much creepier than a foul-mouthed, wretched, rotting right-hander trying to pass itself off as a kid.

In the girl's voice, he says, *"That's not my name, silly."*

The voice sounds as if it's on my left, so I turn in that direction and face the corner. "Yes, it is. Louisa told us. You've been keeping her hostage, and she knows you. Demon, thy name is Azeraul, and you must obey the word of—"

"*Shut up*," the girl's voice screeches. "*I . . . am not . . . Azeraul.*"

"Your lies are pathetic. We know your name. We have power over you."

Mike tugs at my sleeve. "Goddamn it, dude, don't leave me hanging. What's it saying?"

"It's lying," I tell him. "Says its name isn't Azeraul."

"Is it the same one? Maybe the big one left."

I shake my head, feel the earbud wires swaying against my neck, and say, "It's him. I can feel it. Definitely trying to disguise himself."

Mike groans. "God, I hate it when they do that."

I lift my voice to the corner and take two steps closer. "Azeraul. Tell me now. Tell me what you know about Louisa Craghorn."

Nothing. Just that fucking clock ticking like John Henry hammering a railroad spike.

I try a different tactic: flattery. "If you're so powerful, then you must know things that we don't. Doesn't that feel good? Having information? Use that power of yours. Who murdered her? If you tell us that, we'll leave, and you can have your house back. You win, we win."

Silence.

"Was it her husband? Did Dave Craghorn find out that his wife was cheating on him, and he murdered her?"

Excruciating silence.

I'm afraid I've lost him or that he's decided to retreat for now, to regroup and build up more energy before he comes back for another attack.

"Time check, Mike."

"Four minutes, eighteen seconds. Did he ditch? Should we go?"

"Calm before the storm, I think." I move around the love seat and short-step over to the corner where the demon may have been. I don't smell sulfur, nor do I see any signs of him, like floating black masses or darting orbs of light. It's times like this that the full-spectrum camera would come in handy. It's a lesson we thought we'd learned ages ago. You can never have enough batteries.

Especially against a right-hander.

Mike says, "The hair on my arms is standing up."

I look over at him, concerned. "Like, from fear, or what? A presence?"

"Maybe. I don't know. Both?"

Back when the show was running, and even before then when we were two goofy guys with a couple of cameras and a dream, the typical "sensitive" things rarely happened to Mike.

This is not a good sign. I'm worried that Azeraul is sneaking around here, trying to steal Mike's energy from him, perhaps even invade his body.

"Get out of the house."

"But what about—"

"Out the door, Mike. I'll be fine."

"But—"

I quickly remind him about his wife and kids, that he doesn't have to do this, that I dragged him into it, and it's my battle.

He closes his eyes and rubs his temples. "I feel dizzy. Weak, too."

That's even worse.

"Do I have to shove you out that door?"

"My heartbeat is going so fast."

In my earbuds, I hear a cackle of little-girl laughter, like it's the funniest thing she's ever heard. Obviously, Azeraul has absorbed enough of Mike's life force to return.

Mike whispers, "Sulfur," so quietly that it's barely picked up by the microphone. Then he adds, "Two minutes." His arm drops to his side, then the rest of his body crumples onto the middle cushion of the large couch. He sits back, eyes glazed over and staring into the center of the room as if he's catatonic.

I let loose a chorus of curse words and dart across the living room, my shin slamming against the coffee table, sending knickknacks and magazines flying as it overturns. Before I can make it to Mike, I feel a hand on my chest, hot and burning, holding me back.

The little girl's voice says, "*He's mine now, Ford.*"

"Shut up. Shut up. Do *not* use my name. Get off me." I try to wrench away, but no matter which direction I turn, I can feel the pressure of the claw-tipped hand on my skin. "The power of Christ compels you, Azeraul. Get off of—"

The now-familiar screeching roar doesn't just come through my earphones, but it explodes into the entire room, so loud that I can picture it bowing the walls outward.

I trip sideways and fall to the floor, covering my ears. Mike sits, immobile.

Azeraul's voice, as before, comes from everywhere and nowhere at once. "*I am not Azeraul. I am death. I am immortal. I am the enemy of God. I am the destroyer. I am everything you fear, child, but I am not Azeraul. This name you speak has no power over me. Master calls. I must . . . go. Light will come again, but so will I.*"

I can't actually believe what I'm about to do, because it's pure crazy-talk, but I stand up and beg for a demon not to go. "Don't leave. Please. Who murdered Louisa Craghorn? Was it her husband? Did she ever say who it was while you had her trapped? Give me some answers, please!"

Rumbling laughter that chills my spine and sends goosebumps across every inch of skin ripples around the room. And then, words follow that stun me into silence as they trail away, fading into the darkness:

"*Begging . . . beneath you . . . See you again . . . Hopper house.*"

"What the fuck did you just say?" I feel dazed, slammed in the chest by a wrecking ball. "Are you the same . . . the same one . . . the one who . . .?"

And then he's gone.

Azeraul. Not Azeraul.

Whatever that thing's name is, it left the house. Just like before, when we initially drove him back, the room, the entirety of wood, brick, and stone in this structure, feels lighter. Brighter. Almost as if rock and maple alike are heaving a sigh of relief. The suffocating blanket that's been choking the atmosphere has lifted, too, and for the first time since I stepped in this house earlier today—soon to be yesterday, according to the ticking wall clock—it feels like I'm inhaling clean, fresh air. The hint of putrid smoke that laced the oxygen is gone, and I take deep breaths until my lungs feel washed and bleached of the demonic muck.

His final words clang around inside my head.

*See you again . . . Hopper house.*

I don't even—I can't wrap my mind around this possibility. We're along the coast of Virginia. The Hopper house is in Ohio, a thousand miles away.

I stand, completely motionless, considering the implications. It's not unheard-of for spirits to become attached to items and move thousands of miles, and I wouldn't imagine that demons would be confined to an area. It's not like Satan is franchising haunted houses, and these soul-sucking bastards have to set up shop in a specific territory.

But, holy shit, what are the odds that Chelsea's demon is the same one that was here? And that I would end up here investigating it as well? Mike suggested the possibility earlier, but I scoffed at him, and now . . .

*See you again . . . Hopper house.*

Maybe, just maybe, that's not what it meant. Maybe he was saying he'd see me there. Maybe I'm supposed to go back to Chelsea's old house for a showdown.

I honestly don't know.

Is it a sign? Should I agree to Mike's request for the documentary? Could this really be a shot at redemption?

I tell myself not to let those thoughts intrude. My redemption should not come at the hands of exploiting Chelsea's story again.

Over on the couch, Mike coughs, hard and raspy, like it's his first time smoking a cigarette, and his body is trying to reject the filth in his lungs. He leans forward, hands up over his mouth, and hacks until I go to him. I sit down on the couch by his side, fearful that Not Azeraul might still be inside Mike, having duped me with false promises about leaving. But when he turns to me, I can see the real Mike in his eyes. They're uncontaminated, unpossessed. He's looking at me by his own volition.

He says, "Did we get him?"

"To be continued."

# CHAPTER 22

Mike is beat; says he feels like he had a garbage truck run over his chest, then back up and do it again; wants to drive home and go to bed, sleep next to his wife, but I tell him it's probably too dangerous. If he's that exhausted, I don't want him passing out on the way home, crashing, and then dying. I'd be sad, yeah, and clearly I don't want Mike haunting me because that would be a never-ending barrage of practical jokes, missing keys, and general pestering until I joined him on the other side.

We made the pact to haunt each other, and to be annoyingly foolish about it back when we first started this journey together, and I'm quite positive that Mike hasn't forgotten.

Instead of letting him drive home, I convince him to come zonk out in my hotel room down at the Virginia Beach oceanfront. The couch in my room folds out into one of those grotesquely uncomfortable beds, and I remind him that it'll be like old times, back when we were on the road and filming. Me sleeping like a pampered princess with my face cream to keep the cameras and lighting friendly during the day, accompanied by a rejuvenating eye mask and earplugs, skin soaking up mist from the portable humidifier, all while Mike lay in the other queen bed, snoring, drooling, and sleeping naked.

Awkward were the nights when he'd kick the covers off.

In addition to saving his ass from turning into highway hamburger, I let him know that Detective Thomas will most likely want to speak to him again, adding, "What I do now, it's not like the old days where we'd pack up and head back to the hotel for an after-party. I usually spend a day or two with the detectives, answering questions, going over details of my investigation, maybe trying to help them piece together clues if I don't get any direct answers."

"Whatever," Mike says. "Just give me a bed and some coffee in the morning."

As we pack up the rest of our gear—my small collection compared to Mike's ghost-hunting surplus store quantity—I tell Mike what the right-hander said while he was catatonic. I add, "You're not going to believe this, but I think it's the one who hurt Chelsea."

Mike snorts. "You're shitting me."

"Dead serious, dude. It said, 'See you again. Hopper house.' Just like that."

"But that doesn't necessarily mean it was him."

"True, and I considered that, but the more I think about it, the more it feels right. Doesn't it? I mean, didn't it to you? The same type of energy, the same strength? And you know how we always talked about whether or not demons each have their own signature vibrations?"

"Yeah, I guess."

"It feels right. It feels like it was the same one."

Mike works an SB-11 spirit box into its cushioned slot of the storage case. "Feeling is a lot different than proof. You know that."

"There was something else, too, and it didn't click until it mentioned the Hoppers."

A fat rechargeable battery, now lifeless, gets shoved into its home. "And?"

"That laugh. When I told you it was pretending to be a little girl? You didn't hear it, but I swear on my mother's grave, it was copying Chelsea."

"Funny, I don't remember her laughing. Just terrified and crying."

I slam the lid closed on my case. "Low blow."

"Sorry. Old habits."

"Anyway. It was the same one. I'm positive."

We take one more quick look around the living room to make sure we didn't leave anything behind, and as we're doing so, Mike asks, "Does this mean you'll consider the documentary? Sounds like a challenge to me. Fucker is calling you out. Wants to do battle back at the Hoppers."

He's baiting me, ever so subtly, and it would work if I was ten years younger, but my mind is made up. "I told you already, no way in hell am I exploiting her again."

\*\*\*

The hotel room is icebox cold since I left the air conditioner dial on the January-in-Minnesota setting, and I'm certain that Mike is asleep before I'm finished brushing my teeth. Thankfully, and possibly because in here it's as

217

cold as a demon sucking all the energy out of the room, Mike's conked out in his clothes. The snoring and drooling haven't changed. I'm positive there's already a wet spot on the pillow.

With the temperature outside still sitting at roughly eighty degrees, even at two o'clock in the morning and a hundred yards from the ocean, it seems ridiculous to climb underneath the covers, but man, that air conditioner is top notch. So I pull all eighteen layers of blankets that come with a hotel bed up to my neck and shut my eyes.

Sleep has never come as easily to me as it has for Mike, and once again this feels like our glory days. Same old routine. Mike snoring, me struggling to doze off, only now I'm not worried about how my complexion looks on camera, and I didn't bring earplugs because I hadn't intended on having him around for a sleepover.

It's almost a comforting sound, though, because after what we just went through, it's nice to have company. I appreciate having another living soul in the room. The sound of Mike sawing logs is like a nightlight when you're afraid that something might be under the bed.

I try a variety of meditation techniques to clear my mind—tricks I learned and had to use for a long time after Chelsea's incident—but they're useless at the moment. Every time I feel the junk of the previous sixteen hours slipping away and the slow-moving calm of slumber seeping in, my mind spins back around to that thing's voice and the way it imitated Chelsea's laugh, mocking me.

Wherever it may be *now*, it was *here*, damn it, and regardless of whether it was a coincidence or not, I'm kept awake by the fact that there seems to be some sort of netherworld connection that shares information—like a ghostly Pony Express.

Or perhaps information is shared across energy.

"Energy" in the broadest sense, I guess. I'm not talking about, like, electricity or wind power. I'm no scientist, and, in fact, I could barely tell you the difference between an astrologist and an astrophysicist, but what I *believe* is this: everything, from a ladybug to a boulder, from Dick Cheney to a candy bar, from a cup of coffee to a '69 Chevelle with white racing strips, is made up of atoms and protons and neutrons, the building blocks of the universe, and whether it's inanimate or a two-year-old jumping on a trampoline, everything is made up of this interconnected web of energy. It's not necessarily the hum of life, but the hum of *existence*.

Your coffee table may not be alive, yet it *exists*, and there are billions of particles screaming around and around that make that object what it is.

Thoughts are energy. Emotions are energy. A ham sandwich on rye is energy—bear with me here—and *everything* is connected.

I've believed this for a long time, and I've also believed that spirits can somehow share information like it's a phone call or an e-mail, but I've never really seen concrete evidence of this reality until recently.

I chose not to tell Mike that I had already been investigating Chelsea's case again because, for now, I didn't want him to use it as ammo, or a bargaining chip, in his efforts to get Carla Hancock's documentary going. But in a way, I suppose he deserves to know what I learned back at the old farmhouse before I left for this case.

And, amazingly enough, it's further proof of that interconnected, subatomic layer of . . . what, invisible universe juice?

Which apparently exists on both sides of life and death.

Physically, I don't have an ounce of get-up-and-go left in me. My mind won't stop turning, in spite of this, and I'm afraid my thrashing around in the bed will wake up Mike, so I force myself to sit up and tiptoe quietly through the room. The balcony door complains loudly as the seal is broken—plastic peeling away from plastic. I cringe, but Mike only mumbles something in his sleep and rolls over while I'm greeted with the thick humidity outside our room.

I'm only wearing a pair of basketball shorts, and after the frozen tundra of the room, the warmth feels good on my skin. The concrete balcony is pebbled and prickly under my feet. The white plastic chair, still temperate from the day's heat, bends when I sit and prop my legs up on the glass table. I spot a few lights of trolling fishing vessels, along with a tanker or two heading north toward the Chesapeake Bay, and I try to sit peacefully as the waves crash against the shore.

I go over the three visits to the Hampstead farmhouse in my mind again, trying to make sense of the connection to Chelsea, the demon that affected her and Craghorn both, and the vicious, malevolent, but not demonic, entity residing there.

He, the old farmer I spoke with, may not have anything to do with Chelsea or the demon. Maybe he was just sharing information with me.

The first visit, the two Class-A EVPs: "*I know what you want,*" and "*Chelsea . . . Hopper.*"

The second visit, nothing. It happens.

And then, this last visit. Wow.

How did I end up there to begin with?

The short version goes like this: I got an e-mail from a young lady named Deanna Hampstead about a month ago. She said that I should call her "Hamster," because everyone else did, and that she's our number-one fan. Or, rather, she admitted to being Mike's number-one fan, but since he wasn't available on the Internet, she figured I would be just as interested in performing an investigation at her family's abandoned farmhouse.

The thing is, I get about, oh, 437 of these e-mails each week, and it's often a huge burden on my time to sift through every single one of them myself. So I've hired a personal assistant, a young man named Jesse who lives in Albuquerque, to read through them all and pick out the ones that appear to come from actual detectives in need of assistance. He then follows up with a reply e-mail to assess the validity, and if it's a real case, he passes it along to me for review.

I was up late one night after having watched this bogus "Where Are They Now?" piece on some trashy TV show where they once again compared my good name to a certain German dictator from the past—I laughed, but it didn't mean it wasn't hurtful—and insomnia was inevitable.

I decided to give Jesse a break and sort through a few hundred e-mails myself, and fifteen minutes in, I ran across a subject line that read:

DON'T U KNOW SOME1 NAMED CHELSEA?

That sweet child's name might as well be tattooed on my forehead, and I hadn't had a thorough reaming in a good while, so of course I clicked. This is what it said (spelling mistakes hers):

*Dear Mr. Ford A. Ford,*

*I am Deanna Hampstead but u can call me Hamster since all my friends do. I'm 13yrs old. My fam owns an old farmhouse close to where u live. I think. Ur in Oregon now? N E way, that's what your site says. Biggest fan here of GC and was always in luv w/ Mike Long. #1 fan on earth. I couldn't find him on the web, so I wrote 2 u. N E way, u are an inspiration and made me want to hunt ghosts. I went with my cousin Em and we hunted 1 nite. U would not believe what we caught! EVP of a man and my mom sez it's her Papa Joe, her granpa.*

Truthfully, it hurt my eyes, and my head, trying to decipher what young Hamster was trying to say. Kids these days. But I've always had a soft spot for the younger fans since their minds are such clean slates, unburdened by maturity and skepticism, so I continued reading.

*I nvr would have believed it if I hadn't heard it with my own 2 ears. (Y do ppl say it that way? Course u heard it w/ your own 2 ears. How else would u hear it?) N E way, it was SO cool. We listened and he said, "Ford . . . ghostman" and we were like WHAT SHUT UP. And Y is that cray cray? Papa Joe died in 1983. Mom says he was a mean ol cuss.*

Now she had my attention, obviously. I've had plenty of spirits and demons call me out by name, but rarely, if any, who just happened to pass over to the other side twenty-plus years before the show first aired.

*Me an Em—me is Em backward—funny! N E way, we asked him more ?s and all he would say was, "Ford . . . ghostman." He musta said it 8 more times b4 we left. We said, "Ford and Mike from that show, right?" And then he said, "Yes. Chelsea. Danger."*

After reading that, I said, out loud, as a fully grown, adult male human being: "What?! Shut up. That's cray cray."

*N E way, I have it all on tape. I dunno if u would want to but my mama says u should come talk to Papa Joe because it could be important! I think so 2 b/c Chelsea was like the gurl from that live show u did, right? Here is our phone and email but prob don't call after 9 since Dad gets up early for work. Pls tell Mike he's the best ever! And u 2 obv.*

I remember checking the clock, seeing that it was half past 1:00 a.m. and contemplating calling regardless. I was so amped that I had my cell in my hand, finger hovering over the call button, before better judgment prevailed.

I waited until the next morning. I called. I spoke to Carol Hampstead, Hamster's mother, and after a few rounds of, "Holy crap, you're a celebrity! Hon, get in here! We got that Ford guy from that ghost show on the phone," it was fairly easy to get permission for an investigation. Multiple investigations. As many as I wanted, as long as I promised to give them credit or mention the family if I ever got back on television again.

Funny, isn't it? They didn't want their fifteen minutes of fame. All they wanted was to serve me a nice dinner, ask a few behind-the-scenes questions about *Graveyard: Classified*, and to hear their names on television if the opportunity ever came up.

They live less than thirty miles from my home, just outside of Portland. The primordial family farmhouse is another six miles beyond that, nestled in a field and backed up against a small, rolling hill.

And here I am. Sitting on a balcony in Virginia Beach, Virginia, roughly three thousand miles away from that farmhouse, roughly fifteen hundred miles away from Chelsea Hopper's former home, having battled the same demon, thinking about the incredible EVP that I caught on my third visit, and how it's all connected over so many miles and planes of existence:

"*It's coming . . . Chelsea . . . Key . . . Save . . . the people.*"

What's coming? The demon? And was he saying that Chelsea is the key to something? To what?

And what am I saving the people from? And who are these people?

As the orange glow of the sun warms the eastern horizon, I'm left with more questions than answers. At the moment, the biggest one of them all is, should I tell Mike about this?

# CHAPTER 23

Mike and I each grab a handful of blueberry mini-muffins, an apple apiece, and two cups of coffee from the continental breakfast table before we dart out the door. Well, I dart, and Mike drags along behind me, grumbling about how he's not beholden to Detective Thomas, and he doesn't see why he should have to be in a hurry to get to the station.

By the time the buzzing vibration of my phone woke me up on the balcony at a quarter after nine, the detective had already left seven messages asking what had happened, and did we have any information for him. In addition to that, he had some bad news about Dave Craghorn and wanted to discuss things in person. I was to bring Mike, too, since he had become peripherally involved in the investigation.

Before I dozed off, just as the sun was peeking over the horizon, I had made up my mind to tell Mike about Hamster, the Hampstead farmhouse, and Papa Joe, yet as we whip around curves and weave through the nigh-impenetrable Virginia Beach work-commute traffic, it's clear that now is not the right time. There's too much to explain, too many implications to discuss, and I'd have to parry too many of his queries about my stance on the documentary.

Meanwhile, we inhale our muffins and apples while I curse at the other drivers, and I manage to slog through half a cup of the worst coffee I've ever tasted. Frankly, it tastes like demon piss, which I would expect to be a mixture of sulfur, charcoal, coffee beans that have been scrubbed across the anus of a dead horse, and hazelnut.

Mike's grimace when he sips at his cup is the only confirmation I need that he feels the same.

The station is pulsating with activity, more than I expect at nine thirty in the morning on a random Thursday, with hookers and the homeless, old ladies and tattooed bikers stationed throughout, and it takes a good five minutes before the desk sergeant comes back around to his post. I explain who we are and who we're there to see. He's unimpressed. I can tell by the way his lip goes up into a slight Elvis sneer along with the restrained eye-roll that he thinks I can't see.

Sergeant Hobbart—and I so desperately want to make a hobbit joke—points to a row of lime-green plastic chairs along the wall, the kind that are attached by a length of metal on the bottom, and tells us to have a seat, that someone will be with us shortly.

Before we can move to the horrid chairs that look less comfortable than a bed made of cinderblocks, Detective Thomas pokes his head through a doorway to our right. "You two, follow me." There's no welcoming smile, only the hard posturing of a serious man, and it's then that I wonder if *we're* in trouble for something.

He holds the door open farther, and Mike gives the space in front of us a wide-armed sweep. "After you."

We don't go to Detective Thomas's desk, where I expected we would be led, and instead, he points into a bare room, with a bare table, three chairs, and the sanitized glow of two fluorescent bulbs overhead. Along one wall is a giant mirror.

I haven't been in one of these since the wee hours of the morning after Chelsea's attack. "Uh-oh, what's going on?"

Mike groans and says, "Fuck me, Ford. If you dragged me into—"

"Relax," Detective Thomas interrupts. "You're not under arrest. It's just standard procedure since you two were the last to see Dave Craghorn alive."

Mike says, "Excuse me?"

And I add, "Wait. *Alive?* Like past tense? Was he mur . . . mur . . ." I can't seem to get the word out of my mouth. I cough and pretend like I have something in my throat so that the detective will finish my sentence for me.

"Murdered? No. Sit. *Sit.*" He points to the two chairs on the left side of the table, the ones facing the mirror and the camera mounted in the upper corner, and refuses to sit himself until we finally relent.

We do, and the tabletop is cold underneath my forearms. Mike leans back, hands in his pockets, leg bouncing in anticipation.

Detective Thomas grabs the chair opposite from us, spins it around so that the back of it is facing his chest, and sits down, grunting as he does so. He leans forward, arms across the top, clucks his tongue like my grandma used to do. I can't help but feel as if he's disappointed in us for something, yet it's likelier that he's frustrated with the situation.

"Mr. Craghorn," he says, tapping one long, bony index finger on the tabletop, "was found last night at the first rest stop heading west on I-64, swinging from the rafters."

I don't know the area well enough to be familiar with the one he's talking about, but Mike says, "But that's a couple of hours from here, isn't it?"

"Give or take."

I can't believe this. "Hanging? Are you *positive* he wasn't mur . . . mur . . ."

Damn. Why can't I get that word out? I've talked to dead people for over ten years now, both murdered and not. Perhaps it's a different mindset, given the situation, and considering the fact that I was trying to help the poor bastard a little over twelve hours ago. I think—yeah—Dave Craghorn is the first person I've known that's died since Grandma Ford passed six years ago.

Detective Thomas clasps his fingers together, nibbles at his bottom lip, and nods. "Look, I shouldn't even be sharing this with you guys since *technically* the investigation is ongoing—and please keep your damn mouths shut since I could lose my job for this, okay?"

Mike and I nod. Of course we do.

"I just—" He interrupts himself with a cough that's designed to mask emotion that gets the better of him. "It's a damn shame, and I thought you should know. I've been working this case off and on for years now and Craghorn wasn't a friend, but I felt for the guy. Right? Every indication says that no foul play was involved and that it was a suicide. Some woman up from Charleston found him swinging. Nearly gave her a heart attack. According to the reports, Craghorn was wearing the same clothes he had on when I saw him last, there was no luggage in his car, nothing, so it appears that he left you guys and bolted. And this lady, she said in her statement that there was nothing else but an overturned chair. You gotta figure, that late at night, he could've done it hours earlier."

"Or," Mike says, "if someone did it to him, they'd be long gone."

"True, but nothing points to it."

I ask, "Aren't there security cameras there?"

"Nah, not at that one. That particular rest area probably hasn't been updated since Lee surrendered at Appomattox."

"Did they find a note? Anything like that?"

Detective Thomas nods and fishes in his pants pocket, and for a moment, I think he's going to pull out Dave Craghorn's exact suicide note. The butterflies in my gut swoop, swirl, and drop far into my nether regions.

He extracts a pair of black-rimmed, rectangular glasses from another pocket, then rests the bifocals across the bridge of his nose. "Before I let you look at this, did you notice him acting strangely?"

"You mean any weirder than he already was?"

"Beyond that. Out of *Dave's* ordinary."

I frown and tell him no. Mike does the same. I say to the detective, "No, he wasn't *acting* weird, per se, but we both noticed something about him and wanted to bring it up to you."

"Which was?"

231

"You knew about his scratches, right? All the supposed claw marks all over his body?"

Detective Thomas nods. "I didn't tell him to strip down and inspect him from head to toe, but yeah, that shit looked rough. And you think the, uh, the *demon* did that?"

Mike looks at me, I look at him, and we exchange a simple questioning glance, silently asking each other which one should proceed.

Mike does. It's probably better that way. He's more matter-of-fact, where I would lean toward padding what I felt was true, sorta like using the bumpers when bowling, rather than risking the wrath of the gutters. Mike says, "He was hiding something. Had to be." Mike gently strikes the table with the karate chop side of his palm once, twice, three times. "Had to be, had to be."

Detective Thomas rubs one dry, rough hand over his stubble. "Why do you say that?"

"We've been doing this a long time, and there's no way in hell that a right-hander—sorry, an upper-level demon—is going to discriminate against where he chooses to scratch somebody. Craghorn may have been marked up like the bosun's mate got after him with a cat o' nine tails—"

"Nice one," I interject.

"—but his face and neck weren't scratched at all. Any place that couldn't easily be hidden by long sleeves or jeans or pockets was clear. Initially, when Ford and I talked about it, that made me think that Dave might've had something to do with Louisa's death, and he was trying to use this right-hander in his house as an alibi. Six months ago, new evidence shows up, confirming that his wife was cheating, and now he's gotta figure out how to draw the attention away from himself. Demon comes strolling around, stops in for a visit. Craghorn figures that if he can shred himself to pieces and play the victim to a supernatural beast, he'd be the last place you'd look. That was my thought process on the whole scenario, but then Ford told me that he had a clean alibi for Louisa's murder, so that squashed that theory."

Detective Thomas lays the sheet of paper in his hands onto the table and smoothes it out. The small crinkling sound is big enough to fill the room. "Well, it would've been a perfect theory, and, yes, I noticed and thought the exact same thing because I never bought into the whole demon nonsense. At least not until the fucking thing attacked me at Dave's. I went back and tried to find a hole in his alibi. Made phone calls, tried everything I remembered. The people we questioned back then, I tried them, too, but they couldn't recall much. Long story short, I couldn't find anything. He was innocent of everything except for giving in to his emotional pain."

"Giving in?" I ask. "How?"

"Cutting." Noticing Mike's questioning squint, the detective explains. "Self-damage, Mr. Long. Some people feel that creating physical pain helps alleviate their emotional pain."

"Gotcha."

"We got a court order to search his laptop and found entry after entry on some underground website for cutters where they talked about methods and reasons, almost like it was therapy for some and sexual arousal for others.

Initially, all Dave Craghorn did was talk about losing his wife. Some of the people who responded to him called him a pussy and said he wasn't worthy of being around there. Wasn't long after that he started talking about how he wasn't cutting himself, that he had a demon in his home who was doing it to him, you know? Beyond that, for the next few months, he was like a celebrity on those sites. I guess after a while he started believing his lies. He had detailed discussions with people about his rituals, how he used a Ouija board to draw it out, stuff along those lines."

I'm more than angry. I could've used this information before I went into that fucking hellhole unprepared for the strength of what we were about to face. "And you didn't think to tell me this beforehand?"

"I didn't want to cloud your judgment."

"But—"

I can hear Mike's perturbed huff as Detective Thomas holds up his palm. "That's all it was. Nothing more, nothing less. Unconventional methods call for unconventional tactics, and if you had gone in there with preconceived notions about him, then you might have approached it differently."

"Hell yes, I would have," I say. "I would've gone in with a swimming pool full of holy water and an army of Catholic priests."

"Which is precisely my point."

"Craghorn probably wasn't making that stuff up about the séances and rituals, Detective. That's how the dark man showed up at his house. And, honestly, while I don't fault your motives, that's something that would've been fucking nice to know."

Detective Thomas gives us a pressed-lip, understanding frown as he smoothes out the paper under his palms again. "All I can say is sorry, guys. Integrity of the investigation and all that. Next time, yeah?"

"Forget it. No, seriously, forget it."

He slides the sheet of paper over to us. "Here's a copy of the suicide note that was found in his pocket. From what I can tell, it proves you're right about the whole demon-summoning thing. Yet the question remains, who murdered Louisa? We brought you here for a reason, Ford. Did you learn anything new last night?"

As I scan through Craghorn's heartbreaking note, his last words scrawled out to anyone who might read it, I find a tale of misery and the need to connect with someone and any *thing* after the death of his wife. I stop for a moment and close my eyes. A sad man took his own life, and yet, the world continues to turn.

Maybe one of these days, I'll try to communicate with him. Surely that's a soul that won't rest for a long, long while.

The detective asks me again. "*Hey*. You find anything?"

So goes it. Business as usual. "Nothing that makes any sense. Not now, anyway." I had brought last night's DVR tapes along with me, just in case, and I shove them across the table. "Here. They're yours." I'm a few notches beyond pissed at the guy—let *him* sit in a quiet room for hours and review the evidence. "You can take a listen if you want, but it's mostly some random stuff from Louisa's spirit and that right-hander talking shit."

Mike says to me, "Shouldn't *you* listen to that first?"

"Nah, I'm done. Detective, I'll review the video evidence when I get a chance, within the agreed-upon time frame of our contract. I'll let you know if I find anything else." I have two weeks, officially, to get my report back to him, and given the dickhead move he made, I plan to wait until 11:59 p.m. on the due date before I send the e-mail.

Petty? A little, though I feel it's deserved given the fact that we risked a demonic possession. I've never been a doormat, and I have no plans on becoming a possessed doormat, either.

Speaking of, what would be printed on a possessed doormat?

"Hellcome" to our home?

I continue, "However, I feel like if you're going to find any new evidence, anything you can use, it'll be on the audio." And, I've always wanted to say this in a snide, movie-star tone, but I've never really had the chance. I push myself up from the table and look down on him. "Good *day*, sir."

Mike slaps the table and says, "Hell, yeah. Billy Badass," as he stands up beside me.

# CHAPTER 24

It's a quiet ride in the rental car back to the oceanfront hotel. It feels like Mike and I had our moment, together again, and now it's over. I don't know what he's thinking, but I have a little bit of, "Well, now what?" going on.

I have a long flight home, made bearable by first-class seats paid for with points, even though I could afford my own small jet. Truth is, I enjoy the company of my fellow travelers, along with the recognition of "Hey, you're that guy, right?"

I don't hide from my fading celebrity status. The "used to be" doesn't bother me, no matter how much fun it would be to get back to zero and beyond. I'm looking forward to hanging out with Ulie, giving belly rubs and rawhide treats. I'm already thinking about taking him back to the farmhouse to see if Papa Joe will give me any more information.

And when I go to pick him up from Melanie's place, given what Mike told me about her, I may ask her to dinner—you know, as a way to say thanks for watching the Best Dog in the World.

Maybe it's the right time to tell Mike what I know, that I've already been peripherally reinvestigating the Hopper house and Chelsea's tormentor, and that we just encountered the rotten asshole again and didn't even know it until the end. Mike is silent, though, leaning on the armrest, propping his chin up, and staring out the window.

He looks pensive, and I leave him alone. Traffic rolls by. A naval jet carves a path across the blue sky.

I'll keep it to myself for now. I'm still not ready for the back-and-forth about the documentary, and he's not badgering me, so I'm cool with letting this car ride be what it is—a short end to another chapter.

Brake lights pinball across the highway in front of us, pinging from car to truck to delivery van, and four lanes ease into a slow crawl.

"Accident?" Mike asks. "You see anything?"

"Not yet."

"Shit. I better call Toni." He does, and I listen to him cajole her into forgiveness for having spent the night, and for having entertained my tomfoolery.

He actually uses that word.

*Tomfoolery.*

Funny. He doesn't look like he's eighty years old.

Mike Long, Taker of No Shit, King of You Can't Tell Me What To Do-ville, has always been humbled in the presence of Toni, whether she's in the same room or on the other end of the line. I'm sure it would drive me nuts, but he likes the challenge.

When he promises he'll be home as soon as he can and hangs up, I ask him a risky question. "Do you miss it at all? The show, I mean."

He ponders this while we inch forward, then says, "The long shoots, being away, inhaling a cheeseburger between Carla's call times, nah, not in the slightest. Not one fucking bit. What I *do* miss, honest to God, is being able to help people that were afraid. I miss being able to tell a frightened mother or some old lady that they have nothing to fear, that the evidence we caught would make them happy, you know? A chance to say goodbye one last time, or that somebody's nice uncle was there watching over them. That stuff. I miss being able to tell people that the things that go bump in the night aren't all bad. Well, at least ninety-nine times out of a hundred."

"Chelsea," I say quietly. "Number one hundred."

"Yeah. That girl—"

"Mike, man, don't start, please? I don't need another lecture."

"I wasn't going to. What I was going to say was, other than the money . . ."

*Oh, God. Here we go. Me and my big mouth.*

"Which I really need, I'm sure it's our chance at redemption."

Magically, traffic picks up speed for no apparent reason, after having been stalled for no apparent reason, and I nudge the rental faster to keep up. "What do *you* need redemption for? You tried to stop it."

"I didn't try hard enough," he answers, and there's more weight in those words than I've heard in Mike's voice in a long, long time. "One man can't do it by himself. He needs people on his side."

I understand that it's his subtle attempt at telling me I should have been with him two years ago, and not on the side of glory, fame, and television history, but it causes something else to click.

Since the show was forced off the air—since the lawsuits and having my name trashed on every single news outlet—I've felt like I was riding the subway of life alone. I pushed Melanie away and fell into the beds of other women because they were connections that would be with me for an hour, and then I could retreat again. I hired a personal assistant to answer my fan mail because I couldn't bear interacting with too many people. I've worked with dozens of different police departments doing this paranormal private investigator thing, but always alone on night investigations and research gathering, refusing help, refusing to allow anyone to come along.

I don't know why it hits me so hard. Maybe because it's Mike that's saying it. Maybe it's because I finally grasped that I won't be able to take on Chelsea's demon by myself, like I'd planned. Mike or no Mike. Documentary or no documentary.

Either way, that goddamn thing is strong, wherever it is, wherever it went, and whatever is coming, I'm going to need someone on my side.

"You're right," I say, shifting lanes, squeezing between two semis, as I head toward the hotel. "A man certainly does."

We say our goodbyes in the parking lot, the smell of salt air hanging over our heads, poofball clouds drifting west out over the ocean, as Mike shakes my hand, saying, "It's been real."

"It's been fun."

"But it hasn't been real fun." He gives me a thumbs up and steps backward to his navy blue Audi. "Promise me you'll think about the documentary, okay? Carla's not so bad after all those FCC fines. Lightened her up a bit."

I tell him okay, I will, yet I don't believe for a second that Carla Hancock has changed. That cobra will always have her fangs.

As he's getting into his car, I quickly say, "Hey, Mike?" before he closes his door.

"Yeah?"

"Can I send you some audio files to review? I caught something in this old farmhouse back home. Pretty amazing stuff." I leave it at that. I'll tell him what it is when I'm ready.

He considers this for a moment and seems to be weighing whether he wants to get involved again with the almighty Ford Atticus Ford for something other than the documentary, and then says, "Sure. If you send a package instead of e-mail, don't put your return address on it. Toni will have them in the trash before I even know they're there."

"Cool. Will do. You have a safe trip home."

"And you have a good flight. See you on the other side."

I smile because it's reassuring to hear him say our catchphrase that ended every episode of *Graveyard: Classified*.

"Yep." I wave as he drives off. "See you on the other side."

***

I'm late getting to Melanie's condo in the Pearl District of Portland. My direct flight from Norfolk International was delayed due to mechanical issues, so we had to deplane.

I sipped free scotch in the Billion-Mile Member Lounge for about an hour and a half, then was sufficiently tipsy enough to pass out and sleep all the way home. I needed it after the previous night's war against—well, shit, I want to call that right-hander Azeraul, even though that's not its name.

As I parallel park my Wrangler—it's essential to have a boxy, compact vehicle while you're trying to park in this city—it occurs to me that Louisa Craghorn's spirit never actually said, "His name is Azeraul." The demon was enraged enough to insist that it wasn't, too, which very well could've been a complete lie. Although, I suspect that we would've gotten an entirely different reaction out of him if it *had* been his name. I'm talking, like, a two-year-old throwing a temper tantrum, lying on the floor and stomping its feet, only this would be an ancient demon slinging a couch like it's nothing more than a sippy cup of juice.

I'm disappointed that I had my own tantrum and gave Detective Thomas the audio tapes before I took the time to convert them to files I could listen to on my laptop. The investigation is a huge, intense, emotional blur, but I seem to recall Louisa's spirit saying something about love and *her*.

I keep referring to the right-hander as a he, but who knows, maybe it's been a female demon all along. You hear it often in the natural world: the female of the species is deadlier than the male.

Don't piss off the mama bear.

Could be that the same goes for the *super*natural world.

It's possible, I guess. Remains to be seen.

The truth of the matter is, I'm not necessarily looking forward to going up against that festering cesspool of evil again anytime soon. I need to recharge my own batteries.

Is there a better way to do that other than unconditional doggie love?

I submit that there is not.

I walk up the brick steps to Melanie's front door, breathing in that damp, mossy scent of Portland, and before I even rap my knuckles against the red-painted wood, I can hear Ulie's snorting and scrabbling claws on the tile just inside her entrance. Melanie's voice follows, and it's amusing to hear her say, "Ulie! Ulie! Who's here? Daddy's home!"

The scrabbling claws intensify, Melanie eases the door open around him, and that beautiful mutt has his paws on my chest and is licking underneath my chin before I can speak to my ex-wife. "Wow," I say, once I manage to get him back down on all four legs. "How come *you* were never that excited to see me when I got home?"

Melanie is wearing a cut-off tank top, running shorts, and her hair is up in a ponytail. She looks amazing. She's always looked amazing, but maybe after Mike's revelation, I'm seeing her differently—or seeing her like I used to, like the Melanie from wardrobe that made my pulse race years and years ago. She squashes my moment by saying, "I don't have enough fingers and toes to count all the reasons, Ford."

I can tell she's joking—with some truth hidden behind it—but yeah, it still burns. I hide it by asking how Ulie did as he prances around me, tail wagging so vigorously that his entire bottom shakes. She gives me the rundown, and it's pleasant, cordial, but I don't see anything hidden in her eyes that would suggest she is still in love with me.

Then again, I suck at reading people. Live ones, that is.

She tells me it's late, she has to be at the news station at 4:00 a.m. where she does hair, makeup, and wardrobe for two local morning anchors, and that she'd happily watch Ulie again if I needed her to. She hands me his things—chew toy, peanut butter bulb thingy, his doggie bed, and a backpack full of food and his favorite treats. I feel like I'm picking up my child after a court-ordered weekend visitation with Mom.

Melanie tells me to have a good night and starts to close the door. I hesitate for a beat and then decide to go for it. Nothing ventured, right? I launch my hand out and catch it before she closes it completely. "Wait, can we, um, can we talk for a second?"

She opens the door fully, eyes narrowed, giving me a confused look.

"Do you think you'd . . . How about a drink one night this week, Mel? You up for it? Hit up McNamara's Pub like we used to do?" I'm strongly aware of the awkward, pleading smile on my face, but I can't shove it into anything resembling smooth. So I wait, my heartbeat creating massive craters on the inside of my chest as she arches an eyebrow.

"A drink?"

"Yeah. Just to catch up." The words trip out of my mouth. I feel like I'm sixteen years old, asking Amy

Hemmings to prom, who not-so-politely told me, "Get the hell away from me, weirdo."

Melanie cocks one hip to the side and rests a hand there. "I guess we could. I'd have to ask Jeff to see if he cares, but it shouldn't be a big deal."

"Who's Jeff?" I ask, more incredulous than I intend. Mostly because his name is an atomic bomb in my stomach.

"Actually, it's funny. I've been calling him 'Jeff from the control room' like you used to call me 'Melanie from wardrobe.' We've been seeing each other for a couple of months now. I should really get you two together because he's seen every episode of *GC* at least three times. I made the mistake of telling him we used to be married, and now he won't stop quoting your lines from the show. If I hear 'see you on the other side' one more time, I'm going to vomit."

The only thing I can manage to say is, "Oh, right," and I'm intensely aware of the typical Portland rain that has begun to fall.

"He won't mind, I'm sure."

"Yeah, uh, okay. You check in with him, and I'll give you a call."

Feeling thwarted and defeated, while being jealous enough to fight for what I want, both at the same time, is an odd sensation. Like wearing your shoes on the wrong feet.

"Night, Ford. Nighty-night, Ulie. Auntie Mel will see you again soon!"

I can't even begin to explain how sad I am to hear her say "Auntie" instead of "Mama."

I should've known better.

\*\*\*

It's a long night of restless sleep. Too much snoozing on the flight home, too many thoughts running around inside my head, and too much love from an excited pooch who can't relax and stay in one spot for more than five minutes. I consider putting him in doggie jail, meaning out in the garage for a while, but I haven't seen him in a couple of days and I don't have the heart. Rather than fighting my insomnia, I get up, brew a pot of coffee, and sit down at the kitchen table, laptop open in front of me. I send a note to Jesse down in Albuquerque telling him to take the day off tomorrow, that I'll review the rest of the backlogged e-mails.

What I'm hoping for is another revelation from someone like Hamster Hampstead telling me that they recorded their Papa Joe talking about Chelsea and saving some people. It'd be nice to have the distraction. New evidence. Something to point me in any direction other than Melanie's true north. I also curse Mike for getting my hopes up and partially wonder if he made it all up just to get me in a lighter mood before he pitched the documentary.

I find nothing of the sort. Instead, I sift through and personally answer about a hundred and fifty e-mails, thanking viewers for being friends and fans, before I find anything of interest, and it's not exactly what I'm looking for.

It's a short note from Caribou, the waitress at that crab shack, thanking me profusely for the flagrant tip I left her and how it was such an honor to serve her television idols. As thanks, she included an attachment; it's a picture of her wearing nothing but a *Graveyard: Classified* bandana and high heels.

There's a single ray of sunshine. Oh, happy days.

I save it in a buried folder called "Taxes 2015" along with a few thousand similar pictures, and then drain the last of my coffee. Out my window, high up here on the hill overlooking Portland proper, the sun nudges through the clouds to the east.

Finally, I'm bushed, even with a pot of coffee screeching its tires throughout my veins. My lonely, abandoned wasteland of a king-size bed sounds like a good idea, and I think again about what Mike said.

A man needs someone by his side.

"Ulie," I say, waking him up where he'd been dreaming and twitching on the floor. "You just earned a spot on the bed."

His ears perk and he hops to his feet.

"But we're not going to make a habit of this, got it?"

He snorts. Plain as day, that's the dog version of, "Yeah, right, whatever you say."

On the countertop, my cell phone sits next to a half-eaten bagel and an empty coffee mug. The ceramic body of it is plain white, while the handle is sculpted in the shape of a provocatively posed naked woman. It's a hideously fantastic gag gift from a detective I worked with in the past, and I don't know why, but coffee tastes better coming out of it. The mug itself becomes a trigger object for my thought processes—Caribou in all her naked glory, a detective—and it makes me think about Detective Thomas back in Virginia Beach.

I check the clock over the stove. It's a quarter to six, meaning it's a quarter to nine back on the east coast. He'll be up and at the office by now. My brain feels like I'm thinking through that sludge on the bottom of a riverbed, which is why I consider calling him to apologize. I've had enough time to calm down, and I'll admit that I probably went slightly diva on him back at the station. Dude was just trying to do his job. Been there, yeah?

This whole line of thinking sets off my synapses and they go tumbling along like dominoes.

Dominoes that lead to the word 'Azeraul' in my mind.

I look at Ulie sitting patiently at my feet. "So we're back to that again, huh? This demon-not-demon bullshit?"

He chuffs and flops onto the kitchen floor, exposing his belly as he rolls over and closes his eyes. Smart dog. He can sense I'm not going to bed any time soon.

It's not out of the ordinary for a demon to lie. I absolutely *know* this and have been privy to it on a number of occasions. So, I'm not sure why I just blindly accepted the word of that assmuncher back at Craghorn's. It seemed serious enough to be offended, yet that's not necessarily proof that it's telling the truth.

I hop up from the table and head over to a small library of demon and spirit guides stashed on a living room shelf. Ten books total, ranging from two hundred years old to being published three months ago. You never know when you're gonna need to look up some ancient demon to uncover his weak spots. Helps quite a bit when you're tackling these things with some electronics, holy water, a crucifix, and a middle-aged bald guy named Mike Long. That's not counting the crew, of course, but in the heat of demonic battle, those guys are nothing but doughnut-gobbling, coffee-chugging cannon fodder.

I flip through each guide—some priceless, some barely worth the paper they're printed on—being dainty with the ancient ones and hasty with the others. Brother Luther's *Guide to Demons of the Realm*. Herr Bonn's *Twelve Levels of Demonic Ranks*. *Life of the Hereafter*. *How to Battle Evil*.

A half an hour passes and nothing comes up.

Nothing. Not a goddamn thing.

Maybe the right-hander in Craghorn's house was telling the truth.

I slam the last book closed and trudge into my kitchen, totally wiped out, fed up, and mentally berating myself for wasting time instead of sleeping. Even Ulie is completely zonked. His snoring sounds like a Harley swallowed a chainsaw.

I flop down at the kitchen table again, ready to give up, but the laptop is open, and Google is sitting there right in front of me. "Why not?" I mumble. It takes every last ounce of available energy to type the name into the search bar, then it occurs to me that I might not even be spelling it correctly.

I take a shot with the following: A-Z-E-R-A-U-L.

It's what I imagined it would be all along, and that's close enough. If not, then yes, Google, your creepily telepathic alternate suggestion will probably be correct.

There's always a chance that someone has heard that name before, so it's worth a look, but there's no way I'm going to sit here for too long browsing through cult blogs and obscure movie references if that's what it comes to. This is nothing but a half-court, half-hearted, buzzer-beater shot before I head into the locker room.

Game over, bro. I'm tired. Man, am I tired. I do the clicky thing on the mousey thing and make the search happen, hardly able to keep my eyes open and then—

"What the—"

On the screen, listed in the search results, accompanied by a picture, is a different kind of demon.

She's tan, with frosted hair pulled back in a crisp, efficient bun, and looks positively radiant in a gold-sequined evening gown, holding a matching clutch at her waist. She's at a charity event of some sort, according to the caption.

Who?

Ellen *Azeraul* Gardner. Wife of the former mayor.

The deceased former mayor who was supposedly having an affair with Louisa Craghorn.

Dear God in Heaven. It's all connected.

I fly up from the kitchen chair and lean across the granite countertop, grabbing for my cell phone, and in a bizarre act of universal kismet, it's already vibrating in my hand by the time I pick it up.

Who in the hell would be calling at this hour? The caller ID shows a Virginia number, with a Hampton Roads area code, to be exact.

There's no doubt who's calling—and I already have an idea why.

Impatient, I answer, "Hello? Hello?"

"Ford?"

"Detective Thomas."

"Sorry to call you so early. I wasn't sure if you were still in town and forgot about the time difference—"

"Ellen. *Azeraul.* Gardner," I blurt, interrupting him. I'm excited and out of breath. The name comes out in punchy gasps.

"Well, holy shit, son. You chase ghosts for a living, are you psychic, too?"

"What? Psychic? No, I . . ."

"Coulda fooled me. Thought I might give you a heads up, but it doesn't sound like you need it. How'd you come by that info?"

I give him the short version of my morning, leaving out Caribou and the "Taxes 2015" folder, and explain how it was a random act of curiosity that led to my discovery. "I'm assuming it's connected, Detective, I just don't know who did what."

"That's what we're looking to find out. Those tapes you gave us—you caught what we needed, though you didn't know it at the time. Or, as you apparently discovered, you gave us a lead that we absolutely can't ignore. I've got some uniforms on the way to Mrs. Gardner's house right now."

251

"You think she did it?"

"I'll get to that, but first, let me apologize again for not being upfront about Craghorn's history."

"Water under the bridge, Detective. You were doing your job. I get it."

"Not an excuse. I wouldn't put my own men in danger and I can see why you got pissed. I'm at fault here, no ifs, ands, or buts. And besides, after having been attacked myself, and then listening to your investigation files, I realized just how dangerous and careless it was on my part. I'll make it up to you somehow."

"It's certainly not a play-date in the park, but I'm still marking you down for one favor owed."

"Good. Second, I listened to *all six* hours of your audio. Goddamn spine-chilling, Ford, and I can't believe you do this for a living. I wouldn't have a single pair of underwear without brown stains."

"Takes practice. I couldn't be around murder victims all the time like you guys."

"Point made. Anyway, listening to the EVPs, what caught my ear, and what you stumbled on, is the fact that Ellen Gardner, the wife of the former mayor of Virginia Beach, used to be Ellen Azeraul."

"Right. So how's it all connected? Did she kill Louisa?"

"Don't know yet, but I've got a five dollar bill riding on it."

"A whole five bucks? Remind me not to take you to Vegas."

The man has a hearty, genuine laugh. I didn't think he was capable. "The biggest thing, to me, was hearing

Louisa's voice saying, 'still love her.' It's a bit disjointed because she seems to be answering questions out of order, like answering something you haven't asked yet or giving a delayed answer to something you asked previously."

"It happens. There are quite a few theories that suggest spirits are functioning within a different realm of time, and they may be experiencing it as a whole rather than a linear progression but—whatever. What does it mean? Are you telling me—"

"That Louisa Craghorn was having an illicit affair with Ellen Azeraul Gardner? It's a distinct possibility. My theory is that Louisa lied about who she was having an affair with in her diary to protect her secret lover. So easy to redirect attention by having the secretary be with the powerful boss. No brainer, even.

"We can submit your audio as evidence, although I expect the judge will toss it out. Either way, it's enough to warrant bringing her in for a round of questions. Could be the former mayor found out about it and had someone off Louisa, or could be that Ellen was done with her and wanted her gone before she said something. Whatever the case, we'll get to the bottom of it. We may have just broken this thing wide open, Ford. Thank you."

"No problem. I do what I can."

"I'll be in touch. Oh, and don't speak a word of this to anyone. Ongoing investigation and all that. Keep that favor card handy, bud."

The line clicks before I can say anything else.

Dead silence signals the end of another investigation, but there is so much more out on the horizon, out there in the beyond.

I should be used to this by now, but the finality of it leaves me speechless, and if I had been able to reply, I imagine it would've been something like, "Cool. See you on the other side."

# Spirit World Productions, Inc.

Los Angeles, California
555-682-8307
Contact: Dane Argyle

FOR IMMEDIATE RELEASE

**A match made in heaven (or hell) brings America's most popular ghost-hunting team to the silver screen**

LOS ANGELES (August 1, 2015) – Spirit World Productions, Inc., is thrilled to announce that it has begun preliminary production of the most anticipated documentary in the history of paranormal investigations. The film's executive producer, Carla Hancock, states, "We couldn't possibly be more thrilled that the former lead investigators of *Graveyard: Classified*, Ford Atticus Ford and Mike Long, have enthusiastically agreed to reunite for this feature-length film. We absolutely can't wait to get started."

Ford, the *enfant terrible* of paranormal reality shows, recently came under harsh criticism and public scrutiny for the events that occurred on the night of October 31, 2012, when then-five-year-old Chelsea Hopper suffered a violent and ferocious demonic attack during a live episode of *Graveyard: Classified*. The upcoming documentary, according to Ford, will once again focus on the Hopper House in Ohio, where he and the former show's technical wizard and co-lead investigator, Mike Long, plan to research, investigate, and clear the house of any "evil entities" that are present.

Long says, "This isn't about us. It's about Chelsea. It's *for* Chelsea. Redemption. Vengeance. We're going to march in there and take that [expletive deleted] thing down. We want the whole world to see us win."

Barring any production delays, filming is set to begin in early September, and in an unprecedented, enthusiastic, team-powered effort, Spirit World Productions has planned for a nationwide theatrical release on December 25, 2015. Hancock says, "We'll be working around the clock. It's a crazy timeline, and nearly impossible, but I'm confident we can pull this off for the holiday season. We fully expect some terrifying consequences to this paranormal investigation because Ford and Mike Long are going to war with a demon, but what better way to celebrate a feel-good time of the year than with two heroes getting much-deserved payback for a little girl?"

The project has yet to be titled, but set aside Christmas Day 2015 to witness history.

\*\*\*

# AUTHOR'S NOTE

*Dear Reader,*

Hello! Ernie Lindsey here, writing as Desmond Doane. I hope you had as much fun reading the first installment of the *Graveyard: Classified* series as I did writing it. Just like Ford Atticus Ford, I've been infatuated with the paranormal since I had my first experience with a ghost around age ten. It's been a while, so my memories are slightly clouded, but I know what I heard.

Many of my current readers have asked, "Why the pseudonym?" and it's a fairly easy answer. My intent, writing as Desmond Doane, is to keep my paranormal mystery novels collected and focused on a single genre, like having your whole family under one roof.

I tend to write mysteries and thrillers under my own name, but the *paranormal* stories will be contained within Desmond's realm.

Plus, Desmond is way cooler than I am, and it's good to have him around. If you'd like to check out the multiple series and novels I've written as myself, be sure to visit my author page on Amazon or learn more about me on my website. (I give away a ton of books for free over there, so be sure to check out the preferred reader mailing list.)

No matter what name I'm writing under, it's an honor to have you read my fiction. Without an audience, an author is just a person clacking away on a keyboard, making up stories about fictional people. We wouldn't be here without you, the wonderful friends and fans that escape into the worlds we create.

If you've enjoyed this novel, you can help make a difference in its success. An honest review on Amazon does wonders, and Desmond certainly wouldn't mind if you shared it with your reading friends and family members. If you know anyone who enjoys shows like *Ghost Hunters* or *Ghost Adventures*, Desmond is positive they would be entertained by this, too.

My sincere thanks go out to those who helped with *The Dark Man* for their support, encouragement, and many hours of reading early drafts. The biggest thanks of all go to my wife, who kindly endures all the voices in my head.

Thanks so much again for your time, and I'll see you on the other side.

All best,
Ernie/Desmond
2015

# ADDITIONAL READING

*Other works by Ernie Lindsey*

## Novels

Sara's Game
Sara's Past
Sara's Fear
Warchild: Pawn
Warchild: Judas
Warchild: Spirit
Super
Skynoise
The Marshmallow Hammer Detective Agency
The White Mountain
Going Shogun
The Two Crosses

53270326R00159

Made in the USA
Lexington, KY
28 June 2016